Winterfast

BRIDGE OF LEGENDS

BOOK FOUR

SARAH K. L. WILSON

This is a work of fiction. All characters, places, and events are purely fictitious.

WINTERFAST

Copyright 2019 Sarah K. L. Wilson

ISBN:

978-1-9992872-2-1

Cover art by POLAR ENGINE

Map by Francesca Baerald

www.sarahklwilson.com

Direct comments or feedback to
sarah@sarahklwilson.com.

For Cale

Always

LEGENDS

BYRON BRONZEBOW
A good-looking hero who carries a bronze bow. Known in history for his care for the poor and needy.

DEATHLESS PIRATE
Known for his love of treasure and invulnerability and recognized by his hook for a hand and belt of human skulls.

GRANDFATHER TIMELESS
Based in the Timekeepers religion he is known for his high hat, long black coat and golden waistcoat. He is Time in human form subjecting all to his will.

KING ABELMEYER THE ONE-EYED
Known for his single eye and broken crown, King Abelmeyer united the five cities of the Dragonblood Plains in the alliance that lasts today.

LADY SACRIFICE
Known for her loveliness, innocence and sacrifice for the people, she is usually clad in a white dress.

LILA CHERRYLOCKS
A master thief and trickster. Known for her long cherry-red locks, deft skills, and adventurous spirit.

MAID CHAOS
The right hand of Death. Known for destruction, death and the golden breastplate she wears.

QUEEN MER
Queen of the Sea and mother to the Waverunners. Queen Mer is known for her revenge upon man in the form of hurricanes and typhoons and for the shells, scales, and seaweed that she wears.

RAM THE HUNTER
The unspoken Legend. Not mentioned in the Dragonblood Plains except in whispers, he is known for slaying dragons and going insane in the aftermath.

PROLOGUE

"They came down like a flood. People, people with purple eyes and wild tales of salvation. And we took them in and made them one with us until the first dragons came down from the mountains. We realized our mistake too late. Realized the folly of our mercy only after our children lay dead and our homes burned. But we could not remove the people of the dragons, because we needed their blood to quell the scourge."

- Tales of the Dragonblooded

"Swim, swim, boat in the sea,

Swim, swim, dragon in the sky,

Swim, swim soul in the stars,

Swim for me tonight."

- Songs of the Retribution

1: TOO SILENT

MARIELLE

"I think it's time to realize that the Legends – all of them – are enemies," Tamerlan said through chattering teeth.

"They aren't enemies or allies. They are just ... things. Tools. Options," Etienne said, half distracted as he searched a closet and came out with a long fur cloak. He was fastening it around his neck and pinning it with a cloak pin before he was finished speaking. "Can you smell more fur in the house?"

"On the floor above us," Marielle said. The way the house swayed and the boards above them creaked made her nervous, but the air was growing colder by the second and if they didn't find proper clothing they'd die of the elements before the dragon could finish destroying the city by flying with it on his back. "I'll go. I'm lighter than either of you."

"I don't think that you should," Tamerlan objected, but his overprotectiveness wasn't helping. He'd stayed right beside her in the hours since he freed her from the clock, his gaze barely

3

leaving her – as if he was afraid that she would evaporate if he looked away. The sweetness in his eyes was almost too overwhelming. She shied away from it, afraid of what it could do to her while there were still battles to fight and cities to save. While he was still deeply addicted to a deadly magic habit.

"I'm an officer of the Jingen City Watch – or I was," Marielle said, feeling her cheeks blushing even in the cold. She'd never have that title again. She'd lost it when she'd failed to be sacrificed. "I can take risks. I'm not made of glass."

Tamerlan muttered something under his breath – likely a curse by the way his hands tightened around the sword handle at his side. His affection and protectiveness were understandable, but if she let that rule her, he'd stifle the life out of her. She needed the ability to still take risks on her own. He'd have to learn to deal with that if they ... but her mind stuttered over the idea that there was more to their relationship than friendship. Just because she'd spent time in his head, in his past, in his heart, didn't mean that she should expect anything from him. He might just be this obsessed with her out of guilt.

And yet those thoughts felt hollow. She knew him. She'd been with him in his mind. His love for her was real. And so were those burning emotions in his eyes.

She swallowed, not sure how to manage this level of intensity between them while still achieving their goals. It was like lightning bolts were connecting them, sizzling with power and destructive energy. And she loved the way it made her feel like she was tingling from the inside out.

"Why don't you tell me about how the Legends are our enemies while I try to negotiate what's left of the staircase?" Marielle suggested, picking her way through the rubble of what had once been a fine guild house to the stairway and trying to ignore the way her heart seemed to skip a beat when she brushed past him or how he half-closed his eyes as if to savor that barest touch.

Many of the stairs were missing, shaken to pieces by the movement of the city, and the few that were left wavered dangerously, ready to give at a moment's notice.

She swallowed. It had been hard to find warm clothing in the city, even with her ability to smell wool and fur. The Dragonblood Plains were warm enough not to need the heavy clothing of the mountains even in the dead of winter fur was rare. They'd had more luck in finding wool stockings and cowls, but they needed fur. And she could smell it above – the musky scent left smoky tendrils through the air.

"Isn't it obvious how they are enemies?" Etienne said coldly. "They stole Anglarok and Liandari from us."

"I think, they've always been playing us – playing me." Tamerlan's voice was steadier without the smoke, though his hands shook from withdrawal.

Last night when they'd huddled in the corner of a freezing building trying to wait out the shaking and cold, his hands had shaken so badly that Etienne had told him sharply that he had a problem. Tamerlan hadn't denied it.

"Do you still think I'm insane?" he'd asked the other man. At least he knew, even if it did him no good to know. He'd keep smoking until it killed them all – if he had to. And it was shattering him.

"Yes," Etienne said harshly. "But I will work with the insane if that is all I have."

Marielle swallowed, coming back to the present. She was in love with a man who was losing his mind – she'd realized that in the dark of the night. She was deeply in love with an insane man. That should worry her. Instead, all she could think was that there had to be a way to fulfill her promise to him – that she would put his pieces back together again.

"They know so much more than we do about how this world was built," Tamerlan was saying about the Legends. "About where the dragons come from and what makes them rise, about how the Legends were made. They can make us dance to their tune without any way to fight back. That's what they've been doing with me all along. I need them. I need the power they give me, but they're also the enemy."

"Strange thought coming from you, Alchemist," Etienne said. From the moment they'd pulled her from the clock, Marielle had seen that the strange balance of friendship and tension between the two of them. Insanity bred mistrust. "I thought that if anyone was a Legend-lover it would be you."

"Don't mistake necessity for love," Tamerlan said mildly, but there was a bite behind his words. He was edgy without the spice he smoked. It turned him from the sweet soul Marielle knew he had inside to a sharp-eyed desperate man. And yet under that were still those sudden glimpses at the softness of his heart, the sweetness of his soul.

"So, the Legends are enemies," Marielle said, wincing at a cracking sound as she stepped up onto the next stair. She tested her weight, but it seemed to be holding, so carefully, she took another step. "Or, at the very least tools like Etienne says. What does that mean to us? Can we just avoid them now that we have all the other dragons chained again and only this one underneath us to worry about?"

Her voice faltered a bit at the end. She didn't like remembering that they were flying on the back of a dragon. It gave her chills. What if the dragon decided to roll in the air like a fish in the sea? They'd all fall to their deaths.

"I don't think so," Tamerlan said calmly. "And that's why I'm worried. What about that new Maid Chaos we found? What about the new Legend that the Retribution created in Choan to deal with that city? Can they be contained like the others? It worries me how easily the other Legends were found and dispatched. Do you think that Grandfather Time could have killed other Legends that we didn't know about?"

"Yes," Etienne said, and Marielle looked back to see him and Tamerlan with eyes locked on each other and strained expressions. Etienne's lip curled as he said it and Tamerlan sighed so loud that Marielle could hear his sigh even from halfway up the stairs.

"You can hear him," Tamerlan breathed, his face white. "Now that he's back in the clock he's in your head, isn't he?"

"Who can he hear?" Marielle asked, but her foot fell through the wood of the step. She reached out, catching the banister as the stair she was on and the ones below fell from the wall, smashing into the ground below. The banister was shaking, pulling, twisting.

She realized it was about to fall right before it did, smelling the problem in the wood before her mind could even process it. She leapt to the next step, taking the last four at a run. Either she'd make it, or she'd fall, but trying to go slow at this point would be a sure disaster.

She hit the landing with one foot as the rest of the stairs fell, leaving her teetering on the edge before she flung herself forward across the dusty landing.

She sat up, coughing, clutching her ribs. That had hurt.

Below her, the others were coughing, too.

"Tamerlan?" she called, and then belatedly, "Etienne?"

"Are you hurt?" Tamerlan called back between coughing fits while Etienne called, "We're fine!"

Two very different men.

She shook her head. The floor felt … unstable. That wasn't good. Carefully, she pulled herself to her feet and took a wobbling step toward the scent of the furs.

"I'm going after the fur," she called down. "You two should get out before this place comes down on you."

"Jump down and I'll catch you!" Tamerlan offered.

She ignored his offer. He'd always sacrifice what he needed for someone else. She didn't want him to die of cold before they chained this last dragon. They had to think practically. And yet, he was barely holding off madness with a thousand voices in his head, and yet he was taking time to show her kindness. She shook her head. His tender heart left him vulnerable in a thousand ways.

She carefully picked her way along the corridor toward the scent of the furs. The house was in disarray. The residents could have left at any time, but it was likely that the smoke from the fires that tore through Choan was what had prompted them to leave. This upper floor hadn't even been touched by flame, but black soot coated everything. That was the problem in H'yi. Finding supplies was nearly impossible in a city half-burned. Even the districts that hadn't been ravaged by flame were so heavily coated in soot that finding food or water of any kind was nearly impossible.

They were all thirsty. They were all cold. They were all hungry. She needed to calm down and stop feeling like every one of her emotions were untrustworthy and every sensation was a threat to her. It was just hard to get over being in the clock for two months. Hard to get used to having a body again — especially one that was constantly responding to Tamerlan's gentle voice and burning gaze.

She shook her head. She was here for furs. She could sort out emotions later.

But she had a bad feeling that if she didn't sort them out soon then she was going to damage any chance she had of saving

Tamerlan from himself. She knew she wanted that – wanted it almost more than to save the cities of the Dragonblood Plains from *themselves*. Was everything so bent on its own destruction?

It's just that she felt confused by that desire. She kept feeling like she was missing parts of her mind since exiting the clock – like having lost the ability to jump from time to time and space to space had also lost her the ability to keep it all straight. She'd never been so invested in personal things before. She'd thought justice was more important than personal love or faithfulness. And more than that, it was as if having lost the ability to ride around in Tamerlan's mind had erected an impenetrable barrier between them, leaving her confused and frustrated.

There!

She opened a closet. There was less soot in the small, tight space, but there was a thick grey fur cloak – wolf, perhaps – that she quickly wrapped around herself. Reaching in, she drew out a larger one, also wolf, but with more black in the fur and a slight golden hue. That would do for Tamerlan. There was one more – a dark brown robe with a deep hood. Quickly, she grabbed them both and hurried to the window. This must have been quite the guild house at some point. This room had a balcony. She opened the wide soot-stained window and stepped out to the narrow balcony.

"Catch," she called to the two figures below, throwing the fur cloaks down but before she could consider how she might want to get down, her eyes were drawn away to a figure in the distance, clinging to the spire of one of the last towers still standing. From this distance, she couldn't make out who it was but whoever was watching her ducked into the tower the moment her eyes caught him.

Her heart raced as he disappeared. Was it Liandari or Anglarok? Why was he watching from the spire – were they being stalked by a Legend? That couldn't be good. Her throat felt dry at the thought. It would be even worse if it was someone else out there in this ruined city. Someone they didn't know. But no one would stay in a ruin like this – would they?

She swallowed roughly as the dragon dipped so suddenly that her heart was in her throat, her head swimming. She lost her balance, tumbling from the balcony to the street below.

Winterfast

A SEASON OF CELEBRATION

2: ON A DRAGON'S BACK

TAMERLAN

"It will be Winterfast at home soon," Etienne said as they stood outside the building. It was strange how much he whipsawed back and forth between utter condemnation of Tamerlan and companionability. "I suppose it will be Winterfast here, too, but while the rest of the Dragonblooded Plains might fast for two days, we will be fasting indefinitely."

"Marielle said she could smell preserves somewhere," Tamerlan said. He couldn't tear his eyes off the windows of the floor above. The whole structure shook with every step Marielle made. She shouldn't be up there, but he'd sensed the warning in her words when she told him she was doing this. She didn't want him protecting her when she could do it herself. It felt – wrong – after his obsession with saving her for the past two months. He felt hollow without that in sight.

And yet you aren't hollow, pretty man, and this game isn't over. You are still ours, willingly or unwillingly.

Unwillingly today. Though of all the Legends, he probably liked Lila the most.

Be glad you aren't that other one – the pretty one with the black hair. I can hear the lies the Grandfather whispers to him. They are not pleasant at all.

Tamerlan clenched his jaw. Was the Grandfather really whispering lies into Etienne's ears? Or was Lila whispering lies into Tamerlan's ears to bend Tamerlan to her will? She'd done it before.

When have I ever lied to you?

When she tried to force him to smoke and bring her back to the world.

That's good for both of us. Her tone sounded almost vicious now that he knew what was behind it. *Don't be a fool. It would be better for you to succumb to me than to anyone else. Soon, the decision will no longer be yours.*

"Etienne, the Legends," he began, but his attention was stolen away before he could continue.

He felt a tugging, like a sixth sense and he looked up just in time to see Marielle at the edge of the balcony above.

"Catch!" she called and a cloak dropped down from the sky right before the bottom seemed to drop out of both the street and his stomach as they plummeted through the air. He was never going to get used to riding on the back of a dragon the size of a city. He felt his stomach flip. The thought of their precarious position made it tumble like those cloaks.

16

Dragon. Ram rumbled in his mind but Tamerlan wasn't paying attention. His eyes had never left Marielle. He gasped as she slipped from the balcony and through the air.

His heart jumped into his throat. He leapt forward, arms stretched out.

Could he catch her without hurting them both?

Before he could finish thinking it, she was hitting his arms and he clung to her the second he felt her, gritting his teeth as he tried to absorb her weight in his knees and ankles. He took most of it, but he stumbled and they both fell to the ground, tangled up in her wolf cloak. He rolled under her as he fell, taking the hit on his shoulder and grunting as the wound in his leg flared from the impact.

Marielle landed on his chest, her small frame quivering – whether from shock or fear he didn't know. He released her immediately, his hands refusing to hold her unless she willed it. He never wanted to see her imprisoned again, not by him, not by anyone. A flash of guilt rushed through him even though another part of him ached to hold her, to pull her into his embrace.

He swallowed down the question on his lips – the desperate need to know if she was hurt. She hadn't liked it the last time. He had to be careful. He had to protect her from everything – even from himself – especially from himself. If he was really mad, like Etienne thought, then he needed to give her the chance to stay away from him – to stay safe from his madness.

17

He drew in a breath quivering with pent up desire – not for her physical body, oh it was so much worse than that now. He knew that what he was trying to conceal was his insatiable need to have the *right* to ask if she was okay. To possess her heart in the way that made concern for her safety natural, that made sacrificing himself for her normal, that made this obsession of his as simple as breathing.

He let out his breath in a half-whispered apology. "Sorry."

Her hair slipped across his face as she pulled herself up, her face flaring hot and red. He bit his lip at the brush of those silky strands. If he lived only a few more days, he wanted to remember this. If all he could reasonably have were those accidental touches, then he would savor every one.

"Thank you," she said, sincerity and awkwardness warring in her voice.

Etienne cleared his throat. "You were saying something about the Legends being our enemies, Tamerlan?"

"Yes," Tamerlan agreed, shaking his head to clear it, pulling himself to his feet and scooping up the cloak Marielle had found for him. He had it pinned around him and his trembling hands back under control before he looked up to meet Etienne's eyes again. "They're linked to the dragons and the dragons binding is what keeps the Dragonblood Plains safe. So, one way or another, we will have to deal with the Legends if we're going to deal with the dragons."

"Then maybe we should have let Grandfather Timeless kill all their avatars," Etienne said smoothly. His arms were crossed over his chest and his eyes narrowed.

Tamerlan knew Etienne was watching for a response, but he couldn't help it when he flinched from the sudden cursing in his head.

Dragon's spit in a cup! Kill him now! Lila sounded shrill. Tamerlan closed his eyes and kept his lips firmly sealed against the words she wanted to pull from him.

The dragons are the enemy, not the Legends. They must be bound! Bound forever by the blood and magic of men! That raving sounded like Ram, but behind it, more voices were screaming in a tangle of sound he couldn't sort out. It bashed at his mind like an internal hammer.

"Is that you speaking, or the Grandfather, Etienne?" he asked schooling his voice to calmness, eyes still closed. He snapped them open at the last second to see Etienne's response.

"What are you asking me, Tamerlan?" Etienne asked. It was a challenge.

Tamerlan held up his hands, asking for peace. "We are on the same side. We want the same thing."

"Do we?" His eyes blazed and Tamerlan's heart kicked up to another level. Was Etienne going mad, too? Would everyone touched by the Legends go mad now? He could feel his pulse in his neck, pounding so hard he was afraid a vein might burst.

19

"Of course, we do," Marielle said, her chiming voice splitting through their tension. Tamerlan could almost feel his body relaxing at her words. "We want to save as many people of the Five Cites as we can. We want the dragons gone or back asleep. We want the Legends to remain on the other side of the Bridge. That's what we want. Do you agree?"

"Yes," Tamerlan said, but his eyes were on Etienne, looking for signs that the Grandfather had hold of him. Was it possible that he'd been taken over just like Anglarok and Liandari?

"Yes," said Etienne, biting off the end of the word, but his assurances weren't enough for Tamerlan.

He was not taken over. He simply hears the Grandfather like you hear us. Only the Grandfather is less benevolent. Lila sounded wary.

Since when were any of them benevolent?

If you think we are not, then perhaps we have been too lenient.

Her tone in Tamerlan's head was steel and then someone – he didn't know which of them – began to scream in the background. He felt the blood draining from his face as he shook his head, trying to make the internal screaming stop.

It was hard to go insane and know it at the same time. Harder still when you didn't know if it was your insanity or someone else's.

"We want the same thing, Marielle," Tamerlan said as gently as he could while trying to keep the pain of the endless screaming from showing on his face. "Thank you for finding us the furs. Do you think you could help us find what happened to Jhinn?"

He reached down and picked up the second cloak from the ground. If they found Jhinn, he would be cold.

She looked up at the sky, worry painting her face. They were all nervous about the night. Last night had been like a glimpse of hell. No one wanted that again.

"I think there's enough daylight," she said uncertainly. "And we owe him that."

Etienne nodded eagerly, as if he was grateful to focus on something else. Was it possible that he heard the screaming, too?

He held out his hand to Tamerlan. "Peace? At least until we find a way to quell the dragons forever?"

Tamerlan nodded tightly, but he took Etienne's smaller hand in his giving him a firm handshake. "You know I want that."

Marielle had already risen up on her tiptoes, nose in the air and eyes closed. She stood motionless for long minutes like that while Tamerlan's gaze traced the shape of her nose, the curve of her cheeks, the way that her stray hairs swirled in the frigid air.

The chances of any of them living through this mess – surviving a flight on the back of a dragon – were incredibly slim. He wanted to enjoy every moment of life left with her, even if each tiny joy was laced with vibrant pain and dull sorrow.

And the acid feeling of madness washing through his brain.

He could never afford to forget what he was now.

"This way," she said, striding forward over the shaking streets as they followed her.

Tamerlan kept his eyes on her, admiring her certainty as she moved, enjoying her brisk movements and quick steps.

"There are others in the ruins," Etienne said quietly. "I see movements sometimes."

Tamerlan swallowed. It didn't help to hear the other man confirm his suspicions. It made it worse, somehow.

"Not just Anglarok and Liandari," he agreed. "But even if it was just them, we can't leave them alone to ravage the city. You saw what Anglarok wrote in his blood. He needs help."

He shivered.

"Why not?" Etienne said tiredly.

"I remember what it was like to live like a passenger in my own mind – to watch my hands kill and torture and be unable to look away. It was living hell."

"They won't do that. They'll just kill the dragon."

"Can they kill it?"

"Ask Ram. You're the one with him in your head."

They won't. They can't.

"He doesn't think they can," Tamerlan said reluctantly. "Though he's not much of one for explaining himself."

Etienne snorted. "Neither is the Grandfather. He issues orders. He lets me know what he has in store for me. He doesn't explain the whys behind any of it."

They were following Marielle as she set off across the city, nose in the air, face concentrated as she scented for something very specific – their friend Jhinn. Tamerlan didn't want to think about what would happen if they found Jhinn anywhere except on the water – or if they didn't find him at all. What had happened to him in the chaos? It seemed like such a bitter thing that his religion demand that he stay afloat at all times. If he found himself on land – and how could he not in this city? – it would be worse than death for him. Tamerlan swallowed, trying to turn his mind to anything else.

"And that brings up another problem," Tamerlan said. "If the Grandfather is back in the clock, why isn't H'yi on the ground? I thought that he was the avatar keeping this dragon here."

"Apparently not."

"Then who is it? We need to know that."

Etienne nodded.

"Choan was Maid Chaos until she was killed and this new Legend created," Marielle said in a distracted voice. Tamerlan started. She'd been listening? He thought she was too absorbed in the hunt. What else had she noticed? Did she know … did she know he was losing his mind? "Xin was bound by Deathless Pirate. An oddly sacrificial choice for a pirate, don't you think? But he's an odd pirate."

Tamerlan exchanged a brief look with Etienne. The other man shook his head quickly. He didn't know all of this, either. Marielle kept talking as she led them carefully over a narrow, shaking bridge. Masonry fell in chunks from it as they scurried across. Tamerlan swallowed as they smacked against the dry canal below. There was no water there. There was no water, anywhere. His throat was parched at the mere thought.

"Jingen was bound by Byron Bronzebow – sort of. That bond weakened over time though I don't know why. Jingen should not have been able to rise when I was spared death, only to wake up. And yet, the dragon rose. Byron showed no hesitation when asked. He was always interested in defending the weak. Maybe he was made a Legend in a different way. And Yan was sealed by King Abelmeyer."

"And H'yi?" Etienne asked, tension in his voice.

"H'yi was bound by the Grandfather."

"Then why isn't it working?" Etienne asked angrily. "We put him back in the clock. That should keep him sealed. There's no reason for him to rise!"

"Do you think – " Tamerlan began but he hesitated. It was only a guess. And a silly one at that. It didn't make logical sense. But did any of this.

"Spit it out," Etienne said.

Tamerlan cleared his throat. They were climbing up the Dragon's spine now to the base of his neck and the wobbling of his movements seemed even greater here. Tamerlan's stomach lurched with every tilt of the land beneath his feet.

24

Could there really be more people in the city? What did *they* think of all of this?

"Do you think that when the Legends leapt out of the clock and took over Liandari and Anglarok that perhaps they broke that pact? That somehow that nullified the hold the clock had on the dragon?"

Etienne shook his head. "It doesn't make sense."

"What *does* make sense?" Tamerlan asked.

"Water!" Marielle's voice was thick with excitement. "I can smell it just up ahead!

3: So Little Water

MARIELLE

Water always smelled so … alive. It was easy to see why Queen Mer's people revered it. It smelled like life – fecund, thriving life. Even here in the middle of a city that was mostly charcoal, the water was alive.

If Marielle was being honest, the charcoal of the city had been a welcome relief. There was nothing like charcoal to clean the air of scent and her sensitive nose – freshly freed from the clock – was grateful to be able to settle back into constant scenting with a bit of a reprieve.

But at this moment it didn't feel like any relief at all. She could smell the water up ahead, but there was a lot more she was smelling, too.

Fear and desperation pulsed through the air in waves of ginger and acid. The lightning blue of the fear tinging the orange desperation in veins of blue. Her teeth were set on edge immediately, but she couldn't keep her feet from hurrying after it.

She could smell Anglarok in the middle of the street as if he was still there. The smell of insanity weaving through his scent was familiar – Legend. And there were more people scents. At least a dozen. They crisscrossed over and through each other. And they were layered up and over as if some of these people had come here multiple times. Interesting. And a little terrifying.

"Ready yourselves," she breathed, grateful when she heard the sounds of drawn swords behind her. Good. They might need them.

There was the sound of a tiny trickle of water and other sounds – something dull like mud being slapped into place by the handful and the lapping of waves against something wooden.

And everywhere the scent of fear and a scant overtone of smoky red violence. She held her breath as they turned the corner and then sighed with relief when she was hit full-on with the strawberry scent of genius.

"Jhinn!" she called aloud before she'd even seen him, but her eyes found him before anything else.

He was standing with his head tilted slightly as if he was listening to something, but he straightened, wide-eyed at her call. He was in his small boat and his boat was in a fountain pool in the middle of a square. It was large for a fountain pool and the only water Marielle had yet seen – but it was hardly anything to float a gondola on. It was maybe ten times in circumference as the length of the small boat and the edges of the fountain were chipped and broken. It was clear to see that Jhinn was trying to dam it up with debris and mud – but he could only reach what was accessible from leaning outside his small boat.

"You live," he said with a grin as they rounded the corner. Even now, even with despair rolling off him in dark puffs of cloud, even now he smiled. "I knew you would live. I knew this couldn't be the end."

But as he looked around him and up at the constantly moving starry sky, his eyes were full of anxiety. Marielle swallowed. What had she expected? Right now, Jhinn was like a man clutching a barrel in the middle of the ocean with no land in sight.

"It's not the end," Tamerlan said warmly, rushing to where Jhinn was and levering a huge timber up to help shore up a woven wall of sticks and mud.

"It's not full yet, but if I can dam it, then when it rains – if it rains – I can catch water," Jhinn said, laughing as he spoke as if it was the most obvious thing in the world and also as if it were the most ridiculous. "I think it's the only water around. Anglarok came here, but though he watched me like a seagull eyeing a scrap, he only stopped to lap water and then he was gone. Liandari was not far behind, but she was not herself and she barely glanced at me before filling a water skin and then slipping away."

He didn't stop working, even when Tamerlan put a friendly hand on his shoulder. He looked feverish and pale – as if he

28

thought he could work hard enough to keep all the water contained. Marielle watched him carefully. Was he going mad, too, or was he simply a realist? That water in his pool would not last long. Especially if it were the only water source for the whole city.

"The walls need to be high," he said feverishly as he piled more debris on them. "Every time the dragon wheels, a little water sloshes out. If I can just keep it in – just work hard enough to keep it in."

"How can we help?" Tamerlan asked. "Do you need supplies?"

Jhinn shook his head but it kept shaking for too long as if he was hung up on the thought. "Pitch maybe, if you find it. But would that have survived the fire? Wood to heat it. I don't know, I don't know."

He looked up from his work with wild eyes and Marielle could almost sense his thoughts from the scent of fear that permeated them with spikes of electric blue.

"You must be cold," Tamerlan said, offering Jhinn the dark cloak. He had to adjust it over his friend's shoulders and fasten the pin. Jhinn wouldn't stop for long enough to do it himself. And that was why she loved Tamerlan. He thought about whether his friend was cold. He tried to help, even if there was nothing he could do. "Listen. I got you into this mess. I'll get you out."

He made crazy, unkeepable promises.

"You can't get me out," Jhinn said, looking up for a fraction of a second to meet Tamerlan's eyes. "Even if the dragon sets down somewhere, there won't be any guarantee that there is water near. Even if there is water near, I'm in the middle of a city. The canals are empty. There's no way out."

"You could leave the boat," Etienne said, but his tone was obvious – he didn't really believe that Jhinn would leave.

"To leave is death," Jhinn said. "You know that. I couldn't have set a better trap if I'd thought on it for a month."

"How far will you go for your beliefs? For a religion that can't possibly be true?" There was no fire in Etienne's words, though the smell of pity wafted off them.

"It's true, it's true," Jhinn said, balling his hands into fists and hitting them against his forehead. "Even if it drives me mad, it's true."

"Mad?" Tamerlan asked softly, his eyes deep wells of blue compassion. He knew madness if anyone did. Marielle's lip trembled a little at the thought. She could see the confirmation in his eyes – smell it in the elderberry of his scent.

"I swear I saw my brother in the shadows," Jhinn said with an eerie tone. "Is that not madness?"

Marielle leaned on the barrier as she tried to get a better look at his face, but she had to pull her hand away almost immediately. The edge of the pool was slick with a fine coating of ice. It took her a moment to see that the edges of the pool were rimmed with a delicate trim of ice, too. It was getting colder.

If this pond froze over – she'd heard that could happen in cold places – then what would happen to Jhinn?

"Did your brother live in H'yi?" Tamerlan asked.

"My brother has been one of the dead for a very long time," Jhinn said and almost without warning, Tamerlan lunged forward and grabbed him in a sudden hug. Jhinn looked surprised, but he patted Tamerlan's shoulder distractedly.

He pulled back as quickly as it had started. "I'll find a way, Jhinn. I'll get you out of here somehow. And on water. You won't pay with your life for what I did."

"I don't blame you, Tam," he said quietly. It was strange how easily they communicated, as if they could read each other's thoughts. Maybe it was their long months of working together, their similar pasts, their genius minds that worked in opposite but similar ways. "But you should know everything got soaked in the turmoil. I have your spice – what's left of it, but it's soaked through."

Tamerlan nodded. "I have six rolls left."

"Then use them wisely."

"If I find pitch, I'll bring it. What else do you need?"

"I don't dare light a fire. Not in here. Not with the chance of burning my boat. Unless you find a metal brazier. I could use that. A fire would be nice," he said. "And food. If you find any – "

"Of course."

They clasped hands and then Tamerlan turned to Etienne and Marielle. "Food first or do we chase one of the Legends – and if so, which one?"

"Anglarok," Marielle said without even waiting. "He asked for help. Liandari doesn't want help. So, let's go free him."

"I doubt we'll be able to free him," Tamerlan said, looking in the distance, but it was obvious that he wanted to, that he agreed with her that they should at least try.

"We can free him," Etienne said firmly. "Just not in the way we might like. Lead on, Marielle. Show us to your mentor."

Marielle felt her cheeks flushing. If it came to a choice between being an avatar or dying, which would Anglarok choose? It worried her to think that he might not be able to tell them – that they might have to choose for him. She knew what she would choose, what Etienne would choose, what Tamerlan would choose, but her feet felt heavy at the worry that Anglarok might choose differently. Maybe he would rather live- even if it was a life possessed. But if that was true, would he have written the message in his own blood?

A chill swept over her that had nothing to do with the aching cold of the air. This city was haunted by more than the dead of the fire or the ruins of the city's dreams. It was haunted now by those who shouldn't live at all – by the Legends.

Maybe Tamerlan was right. Maybe the Legends really were the true enemy.

4: ON A WHIFF OF MADNESS

TAMERLAN

There had to be a way to save Jhinn if Tamerlan could only think of it. It was a puzzle like any other. He just had to work it through as he strode through the cinder-land that was once the city of H'yi.

He played it out in his mind. Jhinn had to stay in the gondola. Jhinn had to stay on water. He couldn't stay in the pond forever. There was no other water that they knew about in the city. That was all established fact. Staying here, like a rat stuck in a single hole – well, that wasn't a future. That wasn't survivable, never mind livable. Not a valid solution. So, what was a valid solution?

Tamerlan was the one who brought him here, it was up to Tamerlan to find him a way out.

Somehow.

He chewed his lip, deep in thought as he followed Marielle alongside Etienne.

The two of them held back a little, trying not to muddy the air so that they didn't get in the way of her scenting. It was hard to hang that far back. Especially since he couldn't help but imagine a thousand ways that she could be swept away from them before they could get to her.

But was that real, or was it the madness? He was worried that the line between the two was beginning to blur. And yet, he couldn't help the ache that formed in his chest when she was three paces ahead of them, couldn't help the way his gaze constantly sought her, the way his feet always turned toward her, ready to move at her call, ready to jump at her command. Somehow, he'd become hers over the past few months – as much hers as her belt knife or that yellow shell she had received from the Retribution.

"The dragon has to set down soon. It's been a night and a day. Nothing can fly for that long," Etienne said from beside him.

"I would have thought you would know more about dragons," Tamerlan said. "After all, you were the Lord Mythos. You kept one trapped beneath us for most of your life. You stole his magic a trickle at a time. Do you know nothing about the dragon – what he eats, how he sleeps, how long he will fly?"

"I know how to bind it," Etienne said tightly. "Or at least how to keep it bound. I know how to siphon off magic – just enough to use but not enough to kill it."

"Can you siphon off magic from *this* dragon? Maybe you can weaken it" Tamerlan asked and the other young man's eyebrows rose.

35

"There needs to be an open wound."

"Isn't there one? Why would Jingen have one but not H'yi?"

He shook his head, "I don't know. I hadn't thought of it. I was trained early on not to touch the magic of the dragons in other cities. Only Jingen."

"But that doesn't mean that you can't do it, does it?"

He frowned. "I suppose not. But not from here. I'll have to find the rend in the dragon's scales and touch the wound to make a connection."

"Or perhaps you only think that because you've never tried anything else."

"Perhaps."

"And then you can draw as you need."

He looked uncomfortable.

"This worries you?" Tamerlan was incredulous. "It didn't seem to worry you to draw on the dragon Jingen or to slaughter girls to keep that system working for you."

"That was different. That was managing something known and well documented. This ... well, it could have unintended consequences."

Tamerlan snorted and was surprised as Etienne grabbed his shirt and shoved him against a building wall. He glanced at Marielle, but she was distracted, sniffing the air at a crossroads up ahead.

"We need to come to an agreement, boy," Etienne growled. "We've already agreed to work together. We've already agreed that we want the same things, so why don't we try to figure this out rather than constantly sniping at each other?"

"That works for me," Tamerlan said stiffly. It seemed like Etienne really was affected by the Grandfather. He was usually cold as these snow-laden winds, not hot-headed and hasty. "But does it work for the Grandfather?"

Etienne sneered. "I don't know, does it work for Lila Cherrylocks? Or Ram the Hunter? Or whoever else you have in that blasted head of yours?"

Tamerlan shoved his hands away. "They don't control me."

"And the Grandfather doesn't control me."

He seemed like he meant that, though he might not know what he meant. Not really. Tamerlan would have to watch him – would have to be wary of what the Grandfather might push him to do.

Do you really think you mortals could stop one of us if we took you over completely? Lila asked. *You should stop fighting us and learn to negotiate instead. Give me what I want, and I will give you what you want.*

"Then maybe we can find a way to make them work for us, rather than against us," Tamerlan said.

Exactly, Lila hissed in his mind.

"Maybe we can find a way to discover which of the Legends have Anglarok and Liandari," Tamerlan continued, ignoring her. He didn't plan to give her whatever it was she wanted. But

37

they could use the whispers and hisses to gather information. "Maybe we can figure out how Ram first bound the dragons. Maybe we can figure out how to do it again."

Etienne was nodding. "Can you ask?"

"I've asked."

"Ask again."

I'll tell you what, Lila said in his mind with an amused tone. *Smoke, and we'll tell you something.*

But what would she tell them? Would it be something worthwhile?

Maybe. Smoke and find out.

And then he would be down one of six chances to smoke at all.

Keep me – smoke them all with me, and I'll get you out of this city.

That wasn't currently his priority. The ground lurched under him, reminding him how false that claim was.

"Well?" Etienne asked.

"They won't tell me anything worthwhile."

Liar.

"Me neither," Etienne said. Was he lying, too? "So, we go to where the knowledge is."

"A library?" Tamerlan asked, brushing the soot from his cloak as best as he could. He couldn't help the thrill that filled him at the thought of exploring one of the Libraries here unhindered. Would any of them still stand after the fire? And would they contain any books? Surely in the months since the city was destroyed, someone would have returned and raided the books.

Ahead of them, Marielle set out again, heading down a wide street. They needed to catch up with her. They were deep in the Spice District and the buildings here were little more than burned-out hulks. There had been too much inside them that was flammable. Too much tinder for the fire.

"Yes, a library," Etienne said. "And Tamerlan?" Tamerlan spun to look at him as he finished what he was saying. His eyes held a look of vulnerability that was curiously unlike him. "We need to trust each other. We're all there is – the only hope for all the Dragonblood Plains."

Tamerlan hesitated, but after a moment, he nodded. He spun back to the crossroads, intending to trot after Marielle, but her silver cloak was nowhere to be seen.

She had disappeared.

5: Blood is Not Thicker

MARIELLE

A clammy hand wrapped around Marielle's mouth but it was hardly needed – not with the kiss of a dagger at her throat.

"Don't say a word," a voice said, breaking slightly as he spoke. He pulled her backward and she let him. Tamerlan and Etienne were not far behind and they would be here in a moment. Even if they were not, the moment the dagger was removed, she'd be able to defend herself. She could smell the fear rolling off her attacker in waves. Fear, and something else … what color was that? What scent was that? It was faint. Barely there.

Cranberry! That's what it was. A faint scent of cranberry guilt. He wasn't going to kill her outright.

Her attacker spun her around, pinning her against a nearby blackened wall. It crumbled slightly behind her back, not strong enough to fully support her weight.

"Who are you?"

He was young – sixteen at most, skinny and vulnerable. But it wasn't his youth that shocked her. I was his face.

He looked exactly like Jhinn - the same shape to his young face, the same bright edge to his eyes, the same tang of brilliance in his scent. And yet – there was something about the twist of his mouth and the way his breath stank of flagleaf that told her that he wasn't the same. He was on land, for one thing. And Jhinn would never do that.

"I should ask you the same question," Marielle said.

"The dagger does the asking. Now, pretty Scenter. I need you. Come with me. Quietly. I have friends and if they hear a sound from you – one tiny whimper – they'll leap from the shadows and slaughter those two friends of yours. You wouldn't like that, would you?"

Marielle hesitated.

"The dagger's been dipped in Mandrake Oil. You know what that is, right? One tiny prick and your scent will be gone forever – with your life. Care to risk it?"

Marielle swallowed. She might be able to beat this boy in a fight. It wasn't like she hadn't been given basic unarmed combat training. But if he was telling the truth about the Mandrake Oil, then one slip and she'd be dead. It wasn't worth it. She should wait until the odds were better.

She wasn't sure if he was lying about having friends in the city who could attack Tamerlan and Etienne, but if he wasn't, then that was a risk, too. Though they'd be getting a lot more than they bargained for if they attacked those two. She still shuddered at the memories of Tamerlan fighting with the aid of the Legends. He was unstoppable.

"Watch your step. You don't want to trip," the boy whispered, shoving her away from the wall and down an alley.

He led them through the alley to the edge of what had once been the canals. The stink of mud and refuse filled her nose so strongly that she could barely smell anything else as he maneuvered her to a bridge and forced her to cross.

They were in the Government District of H'yi – even the fires hadn't wiped out the gilded pillars and carefully cut stone of this District. Most of the buildings here were still intact, or at least, though they crumbled from the constant flexing of their foundations, they had not been consumed by the fire.

"In here," her captor said, shoving her roughly into a nearby building.

There was no ceiling or roof left on the building, only stone blocks and shattered clay tiles in tumbled heaps across the floors. Whatever had been in the middle of the room was so heavily buried that it would take weeks of work to clear away the rubble and reveal it. But the walls remained mostly whole and one of them Marielle saw a map of the Dragonblood Plains.

Her eyes clung to it, even while she realized she could see other things in the corner of the building – supplies in a heap. Perhaps the boy was using this as a storehouse for goods he'd raided throughout the city.

He hovered over the stack, cursing in surprise, all but forgetting Marielle as she stumbled toward the map. With a shaking hand, someone had added more to the map in charcoal. Like most maps of the Dragonblood Plains, it showed only the five cities and the nearby islands, ending where the sea grew great and powerful. But whoever had drawn on the map had extended the map across the wall to show the eastern shore of the sea. Cities were marked – especially Quavitlos of Mer, rumored to be the capitol of Queen Mer's people across the sea. And the coastline looked oddly familiar. Marielle squinted at it.

Where had she seen that before?

On Anglarok's tattooed skin! This was his homeland. And either he or Liandari – or someone else – had drawn the map on the wall.

"Gone," the boy shuddered from the corner. "All gone!"

"What is gone?" Marielle asked coolly.

"The fuel and fire! The lanterns!"

That meant that one of the new avatars of the Legends now had the ability to start a fire. Marielle felt a tingling in her fingers at the thought. Fire. What would they do with that? Did they still think they could kill the dragon? While it flew with them on its back?

She looked up at the noonday sun through the fallen roof. No matter where they were flying to, they had to get there soon, didn't they? It couldn't take long for a dragon of this size to go anywhere.

43

As if responding to her thoughts, the dragon spiraled, banking to the side so that the ground under her dipped wildly to one side and the gap in the roof above seemed to no longer show the noon sun, but instead, the mountain ranges beyond. They were close. Very close. Was that the dragon's destination?

A loud call sounded in the sky – like the cry of an eagle – but it was no eagle's cry. Through the tunneled vision of the building's missing roof, Marielle saw the distinct shape of another dragon flying nearby. A dragon so large that it must easily equal that of the dragon she rode. And on its back, a muddy city rested like thick barnacles. Algae slicked the roof of the Seven Suns palace and wild, waterlogged vines clung to the broken bridges and crumbled buildings. Marielle gasped at the sudden memory of entering that palace – so large, so intimidating! – only months ago. The Sunset Tower was missing entirely – sheered off somehow in all that had happened since the city's fall only months ago.

"Mer's spit!" the boy gasped, his arms limp at his sides as he looked at the same thing she was seeing.

She took that moment to leap, reaching for his throat.

6: Rajit

TAMERLAN

"She disappeared into that building," Etienne said with a calculating look on his face. "Did you see the boy who had her? He could be Jhinn's brother, they look so much alike."

They'd followed them through the streets and over the bridge into the Government District. Terror caught in Tamerlan's throat. Just when he'd been starting to relax enough to let Marielle be as free as she wanted to be and then this happens! He'd never forgive himself if –

"Tam? Are you listening to me?" Etienne asked. "Do you see signs of anyone else around? Allies?"

Tamerlan swallowed. "There are tracks in the soot leading out from the building. His. For the most part, I think. But there are unfamiliar tracks leading out from that pile of rubble in the alley."

"But they all go away," Etienne agreed. "No one else goes inside. Not without coming out again. So, he's probably alone with her in there."

Tamerlan held his sword a little higher. No need to smoke. The two of them could fight one boy if they had to.

Don't fool yourself. He's one of Mer's and they are all mad.

How were they mad?

Lila?

No answer.

The Legends took far more from him than they ever gave - and that included information.

The world tilted suddenly, leaning dangerously to the side and Tamerlan stumbled as he tried to keep his footing. He was knocked into a wall where he reached out to clutch the stonework and hold on tight.

Would Jhinn survive a move like this? Would his dam hold?

"The mountains!" Tamerlan gasped as the snowy peaks – far too close! Came into view with the dragon's banking maneuver.

"And Jingen!" Etienne gasped. "I can feel him! I can feel his magic so close."

"Jingen?"

And then another dragon flew across their vision, blocking out the sight of the mountains, a dripping, moldering city still clinging to his back and wings.

Etienne's face was twisted in concentration. Was he trying to take Jingen's magic as he so often had before? He said you had to be near, but how near did he have to get when he was so familiar with Jingen?

Etienne fell to his knees as Tamerlan looked anxiously back and forth between Etienne on the ground and door of the building Marielle had been dragged into and the sky where Jingen roared past. Too many dangers, not enough time!

Jingen's cry was like a deadly eagle and his tail whipped so close to H'yi that Tamerlan could have sworn he saw a building dislodge and plummet past them. He grabbed Etienne by the collar.

"Come on, Etienne! Before we lose her!"

The other man didn't move. He'd fallen to all fours now, his hands splayed out over the ruined street.

Should Tamerlan pick him up and carry him? But if he did, then how would he fight Marielle free? Should he leave him? But what if Marielle and her captor had escaped out the back? Then he'd lose track of Etienne, too.

Cursing, he sheathed his sword. This was not a good plan. He lifted Etienne with sheer force of strength, slinging him up onto his back where he could hold one arm and one leg over his shoulders. Etienne was heavy, weighing Tamerlan down as he jogged across the street, hoping to make it to the door of the building before the dragon twisted again and rocked the city with his movements.

City of H'yi Cartography, was scratched on a plaque beside the door. He needed to get in there, but not without a weapon in his hands. He shifted Etienne to maneuver him to one shoulder.

Should he smoke? He could use some supernatural energy right now.

Do it! We'll save your girl. We'll kill the dragons. We'll end this!

That was Ram. But he knew better by now. When called, a Legend had immense power. He wasn't going to give any of them that power. Not unless they gave him what he needed.

He was fighting a battle he didn't understand for stakes he didn't know. How could he win at that? His only bargaining chip to get some answers was himself. If they wanted him – even for a few hours, then they needed to pay something, too.

Isn't it enough that we give you everything you want?

It wasn't enough. Not nearly.

He wrenched the door open and startled when he saw Marielle standing with a dagger at a boy's throat. He looked her over, anxious to be sure she was safe.

He breathed a sigh of relief. She was whole. There was no blood – though she was dirty and rumpled and her shirt was torn across one shoulder. She shrugged her fur cloak to cover herself as if conscious of his eyes searing across her skin and he smiled gently.

"Looks like you didn't need me," he said. She was skilled, powerful, and determined. She really didn't need him at all. And while that made him proud, it also made him sorrowful – because if she didn't need him then why stay with him? Why not go her own way? She, after all, was the Scenter. He was only a hopeless addict. She'd be better off far from him – and at the same time, he'd never ask her to go.

"What happened to Etienne?" she asked. Her dagger didn't even waver from the boy's throat, though he was sweating. She looked beautiful when she as powerful like this – her purple eyes blazing, her dark hair slipping from the braid she wore in little wisps.

"I think he's stealing power from Jingen – the other dragon. I don't know if it's working."

But though he was answering her, all he could see were those purple eyes and that confident stance.

She cleared her throat as if she could feel that he wanted her and it made her uncomfortable. "Remember when Jhinn said he saw his brother in the streets?"

"Yes," Tamerlan said. Jhinn. He needed a way to save him, too. Some way to move water ...

"Doesn't this look like he could be that brother?"

"Jhinn of Queen Mer's people?" the boy asked soberly.

"Yes," Marielle said, hope glimmering in her eyes. She wanted to save Jhinn, too. "Are you his brother?"

"His brother is dead," the boy spat.

"What was stolen from you here?" Marielle asked, pointing with the dagger for a moment to a stack of blankets and other supplies in a heap to the side.

"Fire supplies. Lanterns. And a shell," he said. "A shell I found. It's mine."

Marielle's eyes met Tamerlan's and they opened wider with understanding.

"One of the Retribution was here," she explained. "We're on their track."

"Then we need to keep going," Tamerlan said. "They can't be too far ahead."

He paused for a moment and then sheathed his sword, freeing his hand to fish the yellow conch shell out of his belt pouch.

"This is yours, I think," he said, offering it to her.

She gasped as soon as she saw it. "Thank you."

Her grip was greedy as she grabbed it away, as if she couldn't wait to use it.

"It reflects magic back," she said, her concentration clearly on the shell and not his words. "And I saw ones like it in my visions of the past – Ram was using them to help trap the dragons. Maybe we can use this one for that."

"It's a lot smaller than the one we saw them using in Choan," Tamerlan said. It was a nice thought, but if they'd needed a big one to make a Legend, wouldn't a big shell be needed to trap a dragon, too?

She turned to the boy. "What's your name?"

"Rajit." He seemed sullen.

"And what are you doing in H'yi?"

He shrugged.

"Why didn't you leave with everyone else?"

"Is this some kind of a guessing game? Look, Scenter, I took you to help me find something, okay? Something I'm looking for. Or at least, something my benefactor is looking for."

"And you need a Scenter to find it?" she asked.

"If I didn't, then I would have found it by now. I've been looking since before this city burned. Looking since before the dragon rose into the sky. Looking since before Summernight."

"What are you looking for?" Marielle asked.

"Like I'd tell you."

Tamerlan watched him. He really could be Jhinn's brother. He was just as daring, just as quick – but twisted somehow. Untrustworthy. Although, when Tamerlan thought about it, Jhinn could be untrustworthy, too. Just never with him.

"It might be a good adventure," Tamerlan offered. If he was Jhinn's brother, he wouldn't be able to say no to this. "Here you are, trapped on top of a flying dragon in a burnt-out city – so close to your goal that you know it could be around any corner, and yet so far away. It must gnaw at you. It must make you angry to be so close and yet not to have it." The boy's eyes burned with anger. "And now here a Scenter drops in your lap. And she can find the thing you want. But only if you tell her. It's both a blessing and a curse – and maybe an adventure. And that's what you're promised in life, right? An adventure?"

51

"Who told you that?"

"One of Queen Mer's people."

He spat. "I hate them."

"But not enough to disagree."

He shrugged before looking at Marielle. "Stop threatening me with that knife and I'll tell you."

Marielle took the knife from his throat and took a step back but she still held it in her clenched fist, as if ready to change her mind at any moment.

"It's a book. A chronicle, my benefactor said. Everything known about Ram the Hunter and how he first trapped the dragons, and it belongs to her."

"Put me down," Etienne sighed and Tamerlan startled. He'd almost forgotten about him in the excitement. His shoulder protested as he carefully put Etienne down on his feet. Tamerlan expected him to take a moment to recover, but instead, he spun quickly, his hand shooting out and grabbing Rajit by the throat. "Your benefactor. Is it Allegra Spellspinner?"

"Who's asking?"

Etienne laughed harshly and Tamerlan clenched his jaw. "The man who will squeeze the life out of you if you lie to me."

"Yes," Rajit said. "It is."

"Fine. Then I'm taking over your contract. You work for me now."

"And who are you?" he asked, boldly, defiantly.

"Allegra's benefactor," Etienne snarled. "Which means that you've always worked for me. And now we get to work. Find Marielle whatever she needs to hunt this book. I want it found before nightfall."

Tamerlan swallowed. The book would be good. If the Legends wouldn't tell them what they needed to know, then finding it out themselves was essential. But he didn't like having to trust this boy. He didn't like that he'd tried to kidnap Marielle. His eyes drifted to her again and she stiffened her spine.

"There were no others helping you, were there?" she asked Rajit coldly.

"But you believed there were, and that's all that counts," he said with an impish grin.

Tamerlan felt his temper flare up. Marielle's narrowed eyes were all that he needed to see to know that she hadn't been fooled, but he didn't like that Rajit had tried to trick her. He didn't like this little guttersnipe at all.

More than that, he was frustrated. He wanted to scoop Marielle up in his arms and take her away to somewhere safe away from all of this, and then he wanted to wrap his arms around her and kiss her until she sighed his name.

And yet, the closer he tried to get to her, the more he realized that he shouldn't do any of that. If she needed protection from anyone, it was from the people in his head.

He clenched his fists and closed his eyes fighting the tremble in his limbs that begged him to smoke. The scent of the spice sang to him, reminding him of how good it felt to take in just one breath – or not even good, just necessary.

No, Marielle shouldn't trust him. She shouldn't want him. For too long he'd been a vessel of the Legends, and she should fear him. He was full of the spirits of their enemies and he couldn't even promise he wouldn't give in to them again, not just because he craved the herbs that brought them to life, but because in every action, every movement, they became more and more powerful and more and more capable of taking him by force.

Even now, he thought that they might only be playing with him – pretending to let him run free when really he was their captive. One they could bend to their will at any time.

She shouldn't trust him and he shouldn't trust himself. He needed to warn her of that while he still could.

7: Scent of a Story

MARIELLE

"If they stole lanterns with oil, can you track that?" Etienne asked Marielle. He held Rajit by the upper arm.

Tamerlan had drifted over to the map on the wall, studying it intently. She smiled slightly. Of course, he'd be as interested as she was about that. Any little bit of new knowledge fascinated him.

"No more than I can already track them by their smells," Marielle said. "But I can smell other things here. Preserves. Dried meat. This boy has a collection of food here and we promised Jhinn we would bring him some when we found it."

"That can wait," Etienne said. "Daylight is fading. We need to find the Retribution before they do something hasty."

"No," Tamerlan disagreed from beside the map. "Did you look at this?"

Was he seeing something Marielle had missed?

"Someone vandalized a map?" Etienne asked cynically. "So what? I'm sure there are plenty of destroyed things in the city."

"It was either Anglarok or Liandari," Marielle said. "When they came here to steal, they couldn't help but correct the map to add their lands across the sea. You can see the names of the cities."

Etienne stepped closer, dragging Rajit with him. "And what does that matter? So, there's a map. I've seen these lands drawn before."

"He picked out the dragons under the cities on the Dragonblood Plains," Tamerlan said, wonder painting his tone. "See how the head and tail are drawn in? And the wings sketched on each one. This took time."

"Everyone knows the dragons are real and sleep beneath the city. This tells us nothing," Etienne said shortly. "If they took fire, then maybe they mean to set fire to the city again. Or maybe they mean to set fire to the clock. Or maybe they plan to drop fire into the wound on the dragon's neck to try to kill it. Whatever they do, can only make things worse. They must be caught or stopped immediately."

"Look over here on their side of the world," Tamerlan said. "They drew a dragon under their city."

Etienne froze. "What?"

"And see here in the curve of the tail," Tamerlan said, pointing to the map.

Marielle leaned in close to see what he saw, trying to ignore the prickles of awareness in her skin as she brushed against him and the overwhelming scent of him that sang to her like a deadly addiction. He turned his head the barest fraction toward her, and his lips turned upward so slightly in the corners that she almost thought she imagined it as he breathed her in like a fellow Scenter might.

She could still remember what it had been like in his head. His sense of scent had been so dull. But the colors he saw almost made up for it. Was that how he had noticed this detail she's missed?

"Is that what I think it is?" she asked, forcing her mind to ignore his scent.

"An egg," he breathed. "A dragon egg on the other side of the sea."

"All the more reason to find the Harbingers and destroy them," Etienne said. "We'll return for the food later. Jhinn won't starve in a single day. And neither will we."

Tamerlan paused, head tilted to the side as if he were listening to something that none of the rest of them could hear. Marielle shivered and then felt herself flushing as Tamerlan's face grew red. He could see her watching him listen to the voices in his head and he was embarrassed by that. Did he think that meant she was judging him? Did he mistake her concern for condemnation?

"We learned before that chasing people only leads to disappointment. Besides, we want to save Anglarok – and

Liandari – if we can, not destroy them," he said dryly. "I think it would be better to go after this book that Rajit is speaking of – the Chronicles of Ram the Hunter. The hidden book. They'll be looking for it, too."

"How do you know?" Etienne asked.

"Because the Legends who have Liandari and Anglarok in their grip also knew Ram the Hunter on the other side of the Bridge of Legends. They will want to know how he trapped the dragons. And they will want to get this book before we can. They'll be looking. If we find it first, they'll come looking for us."

"And the fire? The lantern? You don't think that is what they're planning to use to kill H'yi?" Etienne asked with a raised eyebrow.

"If they're planning to set fire to the city, then all the more reason to find this book first. If it escaped the first fire, it may not escape the second."

"Any ideas on where it is, street rat?" Etienne asked Rajit and Marielle frowned. He wasn't going to get anywhere using violence or insults. That was clearly all the boy knew. Besides, if he really worked for Allegra, he would be a trained liar. She had certainly been practiced at spinning the truth.

"If I knew, I'd already have it," Rajit said with a wicked glitter in his eye. "Maybe you should leave me here. I'll only slow you down."

"Keep dreaming," Etienne said, shoving him forward, but sweat was forming on the former Lord Mythos' brow. Had he captured some of Jingen's magic? Was containing it putting a strain on him? Or was the Grandfather's voice in his mind too strong even for him?

"Why don't you let me tend to the boy," Marielle suggested. "You and Tamerlan don't need my nose to find the book. You need to think about where it is hiding and both of you know libraries better than me."

"Just don't let him slip away," Etienne said sourly, thrusting the boy at her.

Marielle took his arm in one hand and led him over to his supply heap.

"Let's put some of that food in a sack," she said quietly. "In this city, anything you stash could be gone before you return."

"It's like you've been here before," Rajit said sourly.

In the background, Marielle could hear Tamerlan and Etienne debating libraries.

"It should be in the palace library," Etienne was saying. "Anything important would be there."

"I doubt it," Tamerlan disagreed. "The Guild of Librarians would never release such a treasure. It will be in one of the more prestigious libraries in the University District. The Timeless Library, perhaps, or Doomsayer's Library."

"Have you ever been to either of those?" Etienne demanded.

"I've read about them."

Marielle tuned them out as she and Rajit filled a small sack with dried meats and a wheel of hard cheese. There was a small oilcloth-wrapped packet of dried fruit they added, too.

"Too bad we can't bring the cask," she said with a smile at the barrel of salted fish he had to one side. "It would be too heavy, and heavy as it is there wouldn't be enough fish in such a small barrel to warrant it."

"Do you think the barrel is small?" Rajit asked, meeting her eyes and for a moment he looked vulnerable.

She nodded, wondering at his change in expression.

"I remember a barrel like this. In another lifetime," he said.

"When you were one of Queen Mer's people," Marielle stated.

He flinched. "I was never really one of those fanatics."

"What do you think of the Retribution – Queen Mer's people from over the sea?" Marielle pressed. She'd always wondered why the Waverunners and Retribution hated each other so much. Maybe this angry boy could shed some light on it.

"I haven't met them, but if they walk on land without thinking it will kill them, then I suppose they might be all right." He snorted. "Do you know what it's like to grow up never leaving a boat? Never running, never climbing, never standing on solid ground?"

"No."

"It's terrible. It's like being dead your whole life," he said. "That's why I owe Allegra. She saved me from that. I'm going to find that book and get it to her."

"Aren't Queen Mer's people all the same?" Marielle pressed. "Why do some live peaceably and refuse to leave the water while others demand retribution from the plains and walk the land to mete it out?"

He laughed. "Is that what they're doing? Good for them. Let me tell you what I know."

"Come on," she said, leading him to follow her. Tamerlan and Etienne had settled their disagreement and were motioning her to follow. "Tell me on the way."

It was strange to listen to his tale as they picked their way through the ruins of the city, clutching their fur cloaks around them in the frigid blasts of wind that tore across the city and grasping for stability at the buildings nearby every time the dragon shifted in the air and sent them flying off their feet. With every movement of the dragon, Marielle felt more and more nervous. Eventually, he would have to land. And what would they do then?

"Queen Mer rescued us from the Orange Wars – the civil wars of her time. You know about those of course," Rajit said. He seemed to almost relax as he told the story of his people – as if admitting they were his people and reciting their history helped soothe his anger. He told it as if by rote – perhaps he'd learned to tell it this way as a child. "So many children were sacrificed to keep the dragons quiet. So many men and women died in bloody battles as the people of the cities revolted against the way the Legends chose to deal with the dragons of their time.

"And Queen Mer – well, she started just as a fisherwoman and then when her husband died and she took over his fishing company, she had dozens of ships and she bought out more and more as the chaos ruled and people turned desperately to anyone who would take the rudder for them. It was too hard for people to brace against the winds on their own. It was too hard for them to choose to buck the waves without giving over to greater hands to set the sails. And soon, Queen Mer's faction was the strongest in the city and when the civil wars erupted in Choan, she stomped them out with the weight of her power.

"But when the city was in her hands, she finally realized what it would take to hold the dragon and the great creature of the sea who had risen against them – how she would have to give her life to do it. She feared for what that would mean for the people who sided with her. Would the people of Choan turn on them when their leader was gone? Would waiting mean the great creature of the depths plucked every ship of hers from the salt of the sea and crushed it?

"So she set them a task – to find the missing story – the story needed to destroy the dragons forever – or at least that's what she said. Really, I think she was just trying to keep them safe. They were to sail forever without stopping until they found it.

"In the years that followed, everything she predicted came to pass in Choan. She gave her life to bind the sea creature and save the ships. The people rose up and killed those left in her faction. And the People of Queen Mer floated on the seas, keeping their vow to her that they would not set foot on land until they found the story. That they would rule the seas and shelter her memory and find the story.

"But after the first generation, when living in the ships became hard, and when they had found every port and every island and spoken to people far and wide in a dozen different languages, the people formed two groups – the 'faithful' and the pragmatic. The pragmatic realized that they could not rule the seas if they never left the ships. They were at the mercy of traders in the ports who could set any price and demand any concession just to provide basic supplies. And their wealth and influence were dwindling. They decided that to fulfill the latter half of the promise – to rule the seas and find the story – they would have to set foot on land.

"The 'faithful' were not pleased. Determined to fulfill the first half of the promise, they decided that to rule the seas simply meant to survive them. And so, they broke away from the others, calling themselves the 'Waverunners of the Faithful', and 'Queen Mer's True People.' They kept searching for the story until supplies gave out and a plague hit them, and then one boat after another, they made their way back to the cities of the Dragonblood Plains, taking up their residence like rats in the gutters, in the canals of the cities and living a parasite life on the populations there, making coin as gondoliers and hauling supplies in their family boats."

"And the story?" Marielle asked, awed by the bitterness in his voice.

"There is no story. Or if there is, then it is long gone. Personally, I think it was just an excuse Queen Mer invented to keep them away until the fighting in the cities was long over. And she was right to do that. The People of Queen Mer – the pragmatic ones, that is, thrived. They filled the shores to the east. They established ports and outposts, forts and trade routes. They are powerful, magical, and dominant thanks to her and her small lie."

"And the Waverunners?" Marielle asked.

"Are fools." He spat. "Every one of them."

"But you are not from over the ocean," Marielle said. "You are from the canals of the Dragonblood Plains."

His smile held no humor. "Correct. Which is why I know enough to hate their fanaticism. Satisfied now?"

"I think I am," Marielle said.

She was watching the shadows, sucking in deep breaths of air and concentrating on every smell. Throughout Rajit's story, she'd seen tiny flickers of movement in the shadows and faint hints of scent – on both sides. If she wasn't mistaken – and her nose rarely was – then Liandari and Anglarok were listening. Tamerlan had been right that finding the right bait was better than hunting them down. And it turned out Rajit and his blasphemous story was also a kind of bait.

"Tell me, Rajit, is that why the Waverunners call the Retribution dangerous?"

"In part," Rajit said. "The other part is that if they ever put their mark on you, they can call you to them."

"Their mark?" Marielle asked, her hand drifting up to the windrose above her heart.

"A map of some kind, I think. And a way to read it. It's magical. They add to it with tattoos, but it also adds to itself and they can use it to call you. They call it a gift, but it's just a tie to bind you to their will. That's why we – why the Waverunners – say never to accept gifts from them. They fear the mark. And they fear what it can do."

As if his words had triggered it, the Windrose above Marielle's heart began to burn.

8: From the Shadows

Tamerlan paused for a moment beside a fully intact building. This whole street was still intact as if the fires had left one small corridor alone. Fallen masonry and scattered items on the street were the only signs that the street was part of a ruined city. The cobblestones still formed a whole street. Swirls of carefully wrought iron around the city braziers still imitated the flames the braziers would usually hold. Along the walls of the buildings, stone masonry was precision fit to perfect points and angles. Carved workings of iguanas and leaping fish decorated the mantles above the doors or graced the edges of stained-glass windows still flashing in place in the afternoon sun despite the ravages done to the rest of the city.

The building beside him bore a copper plate that said, "Legend Bookbindery."

It looked older than anything else on the street – as if the rest of the buildings had been built around it.

"I think we should try the Timeless Library first," Etienne said but before Tamerlan could answer, he collapsed to the ground hands over his ears.

"Etienne?" Tamerlan asked his heart suddenly racing as he reached toward him.

A cry from Marielle stopped him before he touched the other man. He twisted to see what was caused her cry. She wrenched at her shirt, opening the front of it enough to show the Windrose tattoo on her chest burning bright as the sun.

She gasped, swaying where she stood just a pace behind him. He took a step toward her, arms stretched out to help, but not sure what he could do. She looked at him, lips parting with a vulnerable tremble, pain and confusion filling her eyes.

"Marielle? Are you hurt?"

Why was that mark glowing on her chest and what did it have to do with Etienne's –

An arrow whistled through the air, clattering when it hit the stone just inches from Marielle's head.

Tamerlan grabbed her arm, pulling her toward him as he wrenched the door of the Bookbindery open and shoved her inside. A second arrow skittered across the cobbled street.

"Help him get inside!" Tamerlan screamed to Rajit but though the boy's lips moved, Tamerlan couldn't hear what he was saying. The Legends were screaming in his head.

Free us! NOW! Enough waiting! We will *have you!*

Something battered against his self-control and for a moment his grip on himself was lost as Lila stole his body. She drew his sword, but before she could take a step, he shoved her aside, seizing himself back and pulling Etienne by the arm, practically throwing him and Rajit into the bookbindery. They both stumbled through the door, and Tamerlan hurried after them, closing and barring the door behind him.

His breath was puffing out in wild bursts. Who could be attacking them? Was it Anglarok or Liandari?

Free us! We will help! Don't die like this!

He had enough time to glance around the front room, his hands shaking as he fought off another assault by the Legends in his mind. There was a long wooden counter and the floor-to-ceiling shelves of books. It looked like a library – only the books clearly weren't to be borrowed or for sale. They were being displayed – their spines chained to the shelves. He recognized the illuminated pages of Elroth's *Age of the Legends* and Valgariath's *Dragonblooded*. There would be more he recognized on those shelves, too. This was clearly a prized collection. Someone needed to save these books while they still could. What did it say about the people of the Dragonblood Plains that no one had come back for them?

Tamerlan glanced around. Was the room secured?

"Back," Marielle gasped. Her forehead was damp with sweat and her eyes looked wild. She threw her fur cloak off and wrenched her shirt over her left shoulder. Spidering out from the Windrose was what looked like a map tattooing itself across her shoulder in golden light as Tamerlan watched. She bit her lip and red blood formed in droplets along her white teeth.

Tamerlan gasped, taking one of her hands. "Hold on, Marielle!"

Rajit ran to the back and ducked his head through a door. "Leather and snips and workbenches. That must be where they bind the books. There are barrels of supplies and sheets of vellum."

"Can you lock the door?" Tamerlan asked. His hands were twitching. He could feel the Legends trying to grab him again.

Stop fighting us! We are your only hope!

Rebellious child!

"Not to the outside but maybe to this room," Rajit replied.

Smoke or we'll take you by force! Lila threatened.

Had he ever thought she was the nice Legend?

Oh, I can be nice. I can be amazing. But not right now when we need you to do what you are told. If you don't, everyone will die and the world will burn.

He didn't believe her. She was lying to him.

"Lies," Etienne moaned from where he lay on the floor with his hands over his ears. "All lies! I defy you, father of darkness!"

Tamerlan shivered. Was *he* that insane?

69

"There's nothing to bar the door with!" Rajit called.

"Try!" Tamerlan said. He sheathed his sword so he could use both hands.

The sound of breaking glass pierced the air as one of the red windowpanes smashed and the stained glass fell to the floor around another arrow – or was it a crossbow quarrel? No time to check. There were shutters on the inside of the stained-glass windows. Tamerlan hurried to swing them shut and secure them. It left the room black as night except for the glow from Marielle's magical tattoos.

The light from them throbbed painfully as they spidered across her exposed neck, shoulder, and chest.

There was the sound of steel striking flint. Again.

Light flared from where Marielle stood, green-faced, her clothing ripped right off her shoulder and the skin an angry red around the tattoo. She lit a pair of lanterns on the long wood counter.

Tamerlan swallowed. "It's like they are attacking us from every side."

"Who?" Marielle asked.

"The Legends."

There was a *thunk* from up above.

"Stairs," Tamerlan said, licking his lips. They were dry and parched. Drier now that fear filled his veins.

"There were stairs in the back," Rajit said.

Tamerlan glanced toward the rear door. It didn't look very strong. "We need to reinforce it."

He scrambled to behind the counter, searching for something, anything. Hmm. An old sword was under the counter. Warily, he slotted it in a crack between the floorboards and heaved. There was a groan and a squeak as the nails moved in the wood of the floorboards.

Again.

A floorboard pulled up and he wrestled it free, shoving it to Rajit. "Here. Use it to reinforce the back door."

Something hit the front door hard. A shoulder perhaps. Sweating, Tamerlan turned back to his work, wrestling with the floorboards again. Another squeak. Another board freed. He heaved it aside and then paused. There was a small oilskin package placed under the floorboard. Tamerlan pulled aside the oilcloth to reveal a small leather-bound book. A strange place to put a book. Especially one that wasn't chained down like the others.

He shoved the second board at Rajit along with the rusty sword. "Take this. Use it if you have to."

The moment Rajit took it, Tamerlan fell to his knees as his mind was battered by Deathless Pirate, his hands limp and useless at his side. The book fell from his hands.

Stop resisting! I'm boarding this ship!

"Why couldn't it just be Byron Bronzebow?" he asked through gritted teeth.

Haven't you noticed that he's been missing lately?

Missing? What was he talking about?

Do you think that Queen Mer was the first avatar slain by the Grandfather?

That couldn't be true, could it?

The door rang with blows from outside and something smashed the glass on the other side of the shutters.

"They're going to get in!" Rajit yelled frantically as the back door bowed against the boards he was frantically wedging in place.

Marielle drew her sword.

No! She shouldn't have to fight alone. She swayed on his feet, her face pale and sweat forming on her brow.

"It pulls," she muttered. "It pulls at me. It demands a response."

Tamerlan gritted his teeth, forcing himself up to one knee only to be pushed back down to all fours.

Surrender or die, city dweller!

Tamerlan fought back, shoving himself to his feet and swaying there for a moment. His mind was wild as he fought for control of himself.

You can't fight forever. Eventually, you will grow distracted, or you will go to sleep, or you will realize we are right and then we will have you.

"Why do you think Jingen flew again?" Etienne asked from where he thrashed on the floor. "That wasn't for no reason."

To anyone else, it would have sounded like mad ravings, but Tamerlan knew Etienne was answering his question.

"Because the avatar holding him was slain?" Was he hearing Tamerlan's conversations with the Legends? Or maybe Tamerlan had spoken them aloud. He couldn't remember if he had. "But then why take so long? Choan began to rise first! And Maid Chaos was the third one killed." He was saying between gritted teeth as he fought a mental battle for his own mind.

Deathless Pirate slipped through, slamming the book down on the wooden counter and drawing Tamerlan's sword, raising it above his head.

"The Eye," Etienne gasped. "Your Eye must have held it for a while longer."

At least he'd done something – that one thing – and it had been enough to pin the dragon in place for a short while longer. It had been a ridiculous sacrifice for so small a victory, but at least he could point to one thing he'd done that actually helped people.

It filled him with a burst of hope. A feeling like maybe there was still a way out if he chose the right sacrifices.

It was enough.

Tamerlan rallied, shoving Deathless Pirate out of control of his body and seizing it back. He lowered the sword in trembling hands. Why had Deathless Pirate wanted this book destroyed? He opened the cover of it with one hand while Etienne spoke. He was pulling himself to his feet now and drawing a sword in a trembling grip, his slow footsteps taking him to the window shutter as it rocked against steady blows. The last of the glass clattered and broke.

"He must have killed Byron Bronzebow before he got to Choan. That's how we caught up with him. We shouldn't have been able to catch up, but we did," Etienne said.

Tamerlan wasn't listening. He was staring at the first line scrawled across the page.

"This is the Chronicle of Ram the Hunter. These are his vile deeds done for the sake of mankind. May he be accursed forever."

"It's the Harbingers outside," Marielle said. "I can smell them. Their call is impossible to resist."

As if to prove the point, she took a reluctant step toward the door.

Tamerlan shoved the book inside his shirt and hurried to where she stood, sword held out, sweat pouring down the sides of her face. She was fighting an internal battle as difficult as his and Etienne's. He put a hand on her shoulder, trying to give her support with just that touch. It was hard not to do more – not to lean down and kiss her precious lips. Not to tell her he'd spend the last drop of his life's blood for her if only she asked for it. But he didn't dare distract her. Not when this battle was for her life.

"Resist them," he said. "You have to resist. We can't give in to them now. They are avatars of the Legends and the Legends are trying to destroy us all."

9: Trapped in a Bookbindery

MARIELLE

The swirl of smells turned her stomach and stole her breath away. Madness swirled in the air from every side – the madness of the Legends which seemed to burst with pungent urgency every time they attacked the doors and windows – for two people they seemed to be everywhere at once – and the madness swirling in streaks of scent from Etienne and Tamerlan as they battled the Legends in their own minds for control of their bodies.

And pain made her feel faint as the burning of her tattoo intensified. Each time she took a step toward the door, the pain decreased, only to return when she refused to take another.

There was a clatter from above them and the scent of elderflower was everywhere. Were the Harbingers on the floor above or had the dragon's movements simply knocked something loose?

Marielle's windrose gave another flare of burning pain.

"Seas send as you may, wind blow as you may, I am but a ship on the waters. I am but a vessel of justice and righteousness. Though many waters roll below me, though waves crash all around, still I am whole on the peak of chaos, still I climb to the top of the spray."

When she got that mark, that's what they had her swear. She had sworn to help the Harbingers bring justice. She had sworn not to let the waves of life batter her to uselessness.

Well, justice would be brought. Chaos would be quelled. And she was going to start with the Legends. And she was going to free the Harbingers if she could. They didn't deserve this. They'd only been trying to save her when they were colonized by the Legends.

Tamerlan was right that the Legends were the enemy now – an enemy intent on taking every one of her friends and allies from her one by one, stealing their wills, and forcing them to serve whatever grand purpose the Legends had. And she wasn't convinced that they were all working separately. The way that they had knocked Etienne and Tamerlan down while convincing the Harbingers to ignite her tattoo and draw her to them, suggested a kind of coordination that could only come from a common sense of purpose.

She gasped as the pain grew again. She knew she could relieve it at any moment. All she had to do was go to them.

She was going to thwart that purpose. She was going to find some way to bring justice for the generations of people who had bent under the iron fists of the Legends and the powers of the dragons.

77

She clenched her jaw and stole a quick glance at Rajit.

"Be ready. If they break through, we will fight."

"What about them?" He asked, seeming to include Tamerlan and Etienne in his gaze.

"Just worry about yourself," Etienne snarled.

"They'll fight with us," Marielle assured him, but Rajit looked skeptical.

There was a pause in the battering at the door and then a squealing sound as if someone was trying to pry the door from its hinges.

Marielle swore under her breath, but Etienne was already there, a hand on the door. He stood there for a moment and then the squealing stopped and for a moment all was silent.

"Maybe they gave up when they realized we weren't easy prey," Rajit suggested.

"Doubtful," Etienne said. He seemed to have his mind back. His eyes were too-bright but focused.

"They were testing us," Marielle agreed as the pain of the windrose faded. That could only mean they were going to try something else. "But for what?"

She glanced at Tamerlan, surprised by his silence, but his nose was deeply buried in a small leather-bound book. It smelled of long abandonment – not a hint of human scent left on it.

She wiped cold sweat from her brow. Grateful for relief from the agony that had filled her before. Her tattoos ached but that was nothing compared to the former pain.

Tamerlan flipped the pages with a singular focus she'd never seen in anyone else except for Jhinn, concentration pouring from him in waves of jasmine-scented slate. He was beautiful like that with his blue eyes so focused and every muscle of his face tensed as he flicked through the pages, absorbing their content more quickly than she thought she could ever read. This was his love, his passion. If he'd had the chance to choose his life, he'd have joined the guild of Librarians and had his nose buried in a book every day. It was bittersweet to get a glimpse of what his life should have been.

He looked up, suddenly, giving her a quick smile before his eyes were drawn back to the page like iron to a lodestone. It was moments like this that his madness was far-off and the boy he had been shone through.

"I can see why they won't say his name," he said, awe in his tone. "It's all written here, though not clearly. A lot of this is spent cursing him."

"How did he trap them?" Etienne asked. One of his hands we clenched in a fist, fighting and jerking as he forced it under control.

Marielle felt her chest tighten. How much control did the Grandfather have over him? The Grandfather's aim had been slaying the other Legends and taking control. That, at least, was simple to understand. Power was always a likely motive in any crime.

But what did the rest of the Legends want? Why were they so desperate to bend Tamerlan to their wills and rebind the dragons? She felt her eyes narrow. They hadn't cared so much before the Grandfather had started to kill avatars and then suddenly, they did care. Was it only self-preservation? How much could they communicate with other Legends over the Bridge of Legends? Did all of them know what the others knew, or were they keeping secrets even now? Did they lie and scheme with and against one another already?

"So far, it only tells the story of the first people of the plains," Tamerlan said. "They lived happily on the shores of the sea. They had a culture very different from ours."

"Yeah, yeah," Etienne said irritably, his face twisting as he fought his hand while trying to keep it hidden from the rest of them. Marielle smelled a spike of fear in his scent. To her eyes it was like bursts of electric blue were lighting the room. Because he was losing control? Or for some other reason? She swallowed. "We all know that part. They were the people of the shells. They found these massive empty conch shells that were in each city and the citizens would collect them, claiming to hear things from other worlds or at least other lands in the shells. Voices. Singing. Wisdom. Some even said magic. They traded them as far as the mountain cities and across the sea."

"I didn't know that," Rajit breathed.

"Like the shells that the Harbingers brought with them?" Marielle asked, trying to sound casual. Did the shell she was given possess these same attributes? The Harbingers had been excited when she could hear voices in her shell. They'd thought she had a gift. And then she'd used the echo magic in it to replicate the Grandfather's time jumps. Could her shell do more than just echo magic back?

Etienne shrugged. "Perhaps. Or perhaps they were only similar. There used to be one in every city, but they were all destroyed in the age of Legends."

"The book says," Tamerlan corrected, "that first the Dragonblooded poured down out of the mountains, raving about strange creatures and terrors of the sky. At first, no one believed them. The people of the land took them in, awed by their beautiful purple eyes and fine features."

Marielle let her gaze wander over Tamerlan. He didn't have the purple eyes. Not that she would be able to see that anyways. She could see no color at all. But his fine features and straight back and broad shoulders looked exactly like what she thought those beautiful people would have been like. And like him, they brought with them unbelievable tales. She could almost imagine him coming out of the mountains with that same wild look in his eyes and that same tension in every muscle that he carried even now.

"They brought them into their homes and cities," Tamerlan continued, his voice ebbing and flowing as he told the story. Marielle shivered as she listened, her eyes wandering from one barred door to the next. Where were the Harbingers? What were they waiting for? "And for a few years, they thrived side by side. Intermarrying. Working together. And then the dragons came."

81

"Yes," Etienne said nastily. "They came. And people said that the Dragonblooded were responsible and that's why they chose a sacrifice to send to the dragons from among the Dragonblooded."

"The Lady Sacrifice?" Marielle asked coolly, and this time Etienne had the grace to look ashamed. Because she was the one *he* chose to sacrifice only a few scant months ago.

"The first Lady Sacrifice – not the one who became a Legend – but one of the many who gave their lives over the years," he said calmly. "They spilled her blood on a sleeping dragon and it bound him in immobility for an entire night. It was only later that the people learned that if they could spill her blood into his veins it would keep him motionless for a year."

Marielle sniffed. She didn't know if she was angry at Etienne for still thinking that way was the right way, or at herself for preventing it from happening and starting this tidal wave of disaster that had swept across the Five Cities ever since.

"And do you think that tale is really true or only a Legend?" she asked.

Etienne's mouth twisted cynically. "Who is to say it's less true than this book? Winners write history books and they don't always tell the truth."

"And everyone spreads rumors," Marielle countered. "And they don't always tell the truth either."

Tamerlan was ignoring their by-play, though he stood facing Marielle, never even looking at Etienne as he read.

82

"Ram was one of the Dragonblooded and he went up into the mountains to find the source of the dragons."

"There was no mention of that in the secret histories," Etienne said stiffly.

"Maybe they didn't want to remember," Tamerlan said softly, his eyes running over the paper and he began to read out loud. "Hither he went by long journey and cold, pain his companion and death his constant friend. The party of adventurers who traveled with the Nameless One rose through the foothills as winter's hold slowly took earth in her grasp and though the plains were hearty and winsome so the mountains were black with ice and dull with cold and the party suffered sorely under such bereft conditions, turning to local hamlets and woodcutters for any spare mercies they could lend. But yea verily a storm blew and covered all ground from hamlet to peak with snow of such depth as to bury a horse and cover a home. The party grew faint with weariness and cold and set up camp in a hole hollowed out of the heavy snow and it was there that most froze in the night, never to again walk the lands of men."

Marielle shivered, finding her fur cloak and putting it on again.

"A fire here would be nice," Rajit said wistfully. "I don't know how he reads a book like that. It's almost as bad as a religious book."

"It *is* a religious book," Etienne said, examining the fireplace at the end of the room. His head was half up the chimney as he spoke. He was craning his neck to look up it as if their enemies were going to come down the chimney. "What else would you call something that worships a pantheon of heroes and makes blood sacrifices and feasts to them every year? If that's not a religion, then what is?"

"Are you saying that the Legends are our gods?" Marielle asked. It seemed plausible. But it also seemed crazy. They were just people who became immortal. And saved cities. And ruled the pattern of our years and festivals. And took over Tamerlan and made him do horrific things.

She could feel her mouth forming the shape of an "O" as Etienne smirked at her.

"That's exactly what I'm saying," he said.

"And our gods want to kill us," Tamerlan said. "Or at least, they do now."

His nose was out of the book and he was walking around the edges of the room, his eyes studying the books chained to the shelves while he kept the little book clasped gently in his hands. His eyes were hungry, as if he wished to read every one of them, but he didn't touch them. It was almost as if he was afraid to breathe on them. She'd only seen that look of reverence on his face before when he looked at her.

"But this isn't what they wanted before! They only wanted to be free of their boundaries," Marielle said. "What has changed?"

They were all silent. Only Rajit moved. His hands ran along the bar in front of the door as he watched them as if he was nervous about whether it would hold even though there hadn't been an attack in long minutes.

"I can hear breathing," he whispered. "They aren't done with us."

The room felt warmer as Marielle's head spun so suddenly that she stumbled forward a step. Her windrose flared with pain and her feet tugged toward the door of their own volition. Tamerlan's hand reached up to his head, his face etched with immediate pain. Etienne mirrored his pose almost exactly, only with a sword in his hand instead of a book.

Were the Legends trying to take them over by force again?

"What are they waiting for?" Rajit asked, his words getting higher at the end of the sentence, betraying his fear.

Marielle swallowed, getting her sword ready. Everything seemed brighter, hotter, as if her anticipation of their madness was making her senses overly keen. The pain in her chest choked out coherent thought, forcing her to clench her jaw and focus just to make it through the waves of agony without moaning. She could even swear that she was smelling the smoky smell of violence. Maybe she could smell what was happening inside their heads now. The violent smell of smoke grew stronger.

They're at war, and we are the battlefield," Tamerlan said at last through clenched teeth. "It's Ram against the others. He'll never let the dragons go. But in order to be free, the Legends have to let them go. It's not that they want us dead. They want us to surrender. To give ourselves as their avatars. And if we do that, the rest of the Dragonblood Plains will be ruined."

"And Ram? What does he want?" Etienne asked. His hand spasmed wildly, reaching toward the barred window beside him. "Why this obsession with dragons so many centuries since he bound them?"

Tamerlan shook his head. "It feels – ongoing – like he never stopped fighting. Like it was never really over."

"Do you think it's the egg?" Marielle asked and they both turned their eyes on her. Her eyes narrowed as she fought another spasm of pain, tugging her toward the door.

"Egg?" Etienne asked.

"The breathing has stopped," Rajit announced, freezing beside the door.

"The one that they drew on the map next to their city," Marielle said, clutching one hand to her chest. "The dragon egg. Maybe he won't rest because there's still a dragon out there who isn't bound."

"If it hasn't hatched in centuries then I doubt it will hatch now," Etienne said dryly.

Rajit's eyes sought hers across the room, as if he was trying to tell her with only his gaze that he was panicking.

"Maybe it just needs the right conditions," Marielle said. She shook her head at Rajit. They needed to help him calm down. A jumpy ally was no ally at all.

Etienne snorted. "And it hasn't found them in all these years?"

86

"Do you smell something?" Tamerlan said, shoving the hidden book in his shirt. He was half-way down one of the aisles of books, frozen over one shelf as if he had been studying that book. Which one had taken his interest so strongly? They must be priceless to have been chained here. But it was as if her mind was trying to tell her something about them. Something about how they hadn't burned. Tamerlan's brow was wrinkled with worry. "Smoke, do you smell smoke?"

Marielle gasped. The books. It wasn't that they hadn't burned. It was that they *were* burning.

"The back! Have they lit the back on fire?" she asked at the same time that Rajit gave a panicked yell.

"Wait!" she cried, throwing up a hand, but it was too late.

The boy was already pulling the bar off the front door and yanking it open.

Fire burst through the cracks around the back door as if the cold air rushing in from the front had called it. It leapt through the cracks with a *fump*, searing the books on the nearest shelves. They lit instantly, the fire jumping from book to book to book until it was surrounding them at the same time that Rajit screamed again.

Marielle spun, sword in hand, barely fast enough to deflect the slash aimed at her by a shadowy figure.

She recognized Anglarok's haunted eyes immediately as she tried to recover her balance, barely catching it and getting her sword back up into a second defensive form before his next flurry of attacks rained down. Behind him, Liandari lunged through the smoke, fighting Tamerlan and Etienne both at once, her sword flying through the forms like it was a race.

"Anglarok? It's me! Marielle!"

His face was blank, as if he didn't know who she was, or simply didn't care.

"We want to get you free! We're trying to find a way!"

The Harbingers were outnumbered two to one, and yet Marielle was the one who felt outnumbered.

She saw Tamerlan from the corner of her eye, reaching for his sleeve with his spare hand while the other blocked a blow.

"Don't do it, Tamerlan!" she yelled, distracted enough that she fumbled her block. Anglarok's steel bit into the side of her calf and she groaned. It was only a nick, but he was already turning the sword back in a new lightning-fast attack.

She clenched her teeth, forgot Tamerlan and brought her sword up with both hands on the grip. She didn't dare lose focus in this moment or she'd be destroyed.

She flowed through the sword forms with every form she knew, one ragged clash leading into the next. He was far better than her. For each of her successful defenses, he rained down two more attacks. She was backing up almost into the flames, feeling the heat searing the fur of her cloak. The smell of burning hair mixed with the ashes of books as they blew through the room and out into the street.

In the doorway, there was no sign of Rajit anymore. The fool had let both the enemy and the fire in with that single choice to flee when his nerve broke.

She gritted her teeth and tried not to think about that, or about what he might do Jhinn if he found him in the city. Based on what he'd said about the Waverunners she doubted he'd respect the other boy's religious views. There was something twisted about him – like he'd suffered too many things and been pulled in too many directions for one so young.

Anglarok's lips were moving.

They formed the words "help me" in a silent plea before he was fighting her again, raining blows so fast and hard that her arms rang from trying to deflect them all aside.

Marielle stumbled, falling to the floor, weapon raised desperately above her head. Anglarok raised his sword. With his height advantage, he was going to smash hers. She gritted her teeth, bracing herself. She couldn't retreat, not with flames dancing across the bookshelf behind her and the roar of the fires behind that. She thought her cloak might be close to catching flame already.

If they didn't leave this building, they would all die here.

Anglarok's expression looked torn, like he was warring with himself and then, out of nowhere he was shoved aside.

"Run, Marielle!" Tamerlan said, looking for a brief moment at her with his good eye before turning back to the fight. It was actually him, not one of the Legends. He must not have smoked!

Shocked, she felt like she was frozen in place. He'd listened to her. He'd actually had the strength to resist in a crisis. She hadn't even thought that was possible. His yell of pain shook her back to reality. Anglarok had both hands around Tamerlan's neck as Tamerlan loomed over him. He smashed a fist into Anglarok's face, but the man held on. Hit again, and again, Anglarok bucked under the blow, but his hands were clamped around Tamerlan's throat and Tamerlan's breath was gone, his face red.

Marielle shook herself, pulling herself to her feet and with a cry she ran forward, driving her sword toward Anglarok. He shifted an instant before it drove through his midsection, preventing it from skewering him, though she smelled blood where it rent his clothing and sliced through the skin of his abdomen.

His grip on Tamerlan fell away Tamerlan threw himself backward, clutching at his throat with his free hand and coughing, gasping for air.

Something behind them crashed and Marielle shot forward, grabbing Tamerlan's arm and pulling him to the door.

The smoke was thick and cloying. She coughed trying to clear her lungs, her senses swimming in the scent of smoke and blood and violence all tangled together. She couldn't see Etienne or Liandari. She'd lost track of both of them in the fight. A boom shook the building – something in the backroom or maybe the floor above had fallen hard enough to shake the whole building – and with the shake, they stumbled out onto the street in a gust of smoke and ash.

10: STALKED THROUGH THE SHADOWS

TAMERLAN

Let us free! Lila snarled. She nearly had him as they ran through the door, seizing his momentary panic that he hadn't gotten Marielle out in time and using it as a way to find his weakness.

He felt the tendrils of her mind wrapping around his, seeking for one pressure point in which to squeeze and wrest control from him. There was nothing more invasive than someone in the mind, squeezing, manipulating, deceiving. Sometimes he wondered if his thoughts were even his anymore.

Fool! You were willing to do this before to save her! You let us out! You let us play! You didn't weigh the costs then.

Didn't he? He knew the costs. He knew how great the need must be before he called them again.

All that sacrifice to save her time after time and you nearly lost her in a fire because you won't call us! Doubly the fool! Cursed in your mind. Weak as a new-hatched chick!

But if he was so weak, then why was she so angry. There were two things he still knew: first, that he loved Marielle more than his own life. And second, that he must do whatever was necessary to keep the Legends caged.

Fury tore through his mind, leaving runnels of pain that made him feel like he was burning from the inside out. He wanted to scream. He wanted to cut his own skull open just to let the pain out. He wanted ...

Something crashed into his back and he spun protectively, bringing his sword up. Marielle would go free. Whatever this took, she would! The Legends would not prevail!

It was Etienne's back that had crashed into him. He was still battling Liandari and holding his own over the cobblestones of the street.

Tamerlan – already dazed – could barely keep track of where their swords were, they moved so fast.

Tamerlan stumbled back from the other man, falling into a defensive stance at the same moment that Liandari's sword plunged to the exact place where his head had been only a moment before. She was fighting differently than he remembered – almost like he did now, as if trying to compensate for missing half her vision.

Etienne whipped out a furious counterattack, gaining a step of ground, but she was too fast. She struck again and he barely turned her blade. They needed to get out of there – and fast. Where had that traitor Rajit gone?

When Tamerlan found him, he was going to shake some sense into that fool. If they hadn't found the little book before the Bindery burned, they would have lost everything in that one fool move of his – they might still lose it if they didn't win this skirmish against the Harbingers – or perhaps he should say, the Legends.

Tamerlan checked over his shoulder to see only a silhouette of Marielle looking at something in the sky. Something huge and white and very near. No time to see more. She was safe, at least. He spun back bringing up his own sword, relief surging through his veins that she was okay. As long as she lived and was whole and safe, that was all he asked for.

All? Then LET US IN!

Another hammering shook him internally as this time Deathless Pirate tried to seize him. He was dirty in his tricks, hitting Tamerlan with mental blows and making his hands and feet jerk against his control.

He watched helplessly as Etienne and Liandari fought, his own internal battle rendering him useless.

Liandari darted in with a lightning-quick attack. Etienne countered it, but as his blade turned the edge of hers, he leapt suddenly forward, almost suicidal in his audacity. That wasn't like Etienne. That was like the Grandfather. He hopped suddenly from in front of Liandari to behind her – time not a constraint – and flung out a hand, blasting something like a burst of wind from his palm and into Anglarok behind him. Anglarok was finally stumbling through the door of the building, still tangled in smoke, his cloak on fire around the edges. Etienne's blast threw him down the street to where he landed in a heap on the ground. Smoke poured up in the air in a yellow-tinged pillar, but the fire seemed to be out.

Tamerlan's heart was beating so fast that he thought he was going to choke on it. Liandari's blade whipped toward him and he managed to seize control of his own hands just in time to bring up his guard. He barely shoved her attack aside, using all his strength as a substitute for her superior skill. She spinned away, whirling to attack Etienne and then back again to Tamerlan.

"Abelmeyer," he gasped as he countered the strike, finally getting a chance to lean in with an attack of his own. Deathless Pirate's worst had come and gone, and he was mentally free again – for now. Why didn't Etienne blast Liandari, too? Maybe he'd used up every scrap of magic that he had stolen in that single burst.

A waste.

But that was the Legends for you. They cared nothing for frugality or caution. They only saw the goal of the moment and lunged for it.

It's been good for you all this time, pretty. You shouldn't judge us now. We've been good friends. We could be far worse enemies.

"How did you know it was me?" Liandari asked, but the glitter in her eye told him he'd guessed correctly. Abelmeyer was in her mind, controlling her actions like she was nothing more than a cloak thrown 'round his shoulders.

"You fight like a man with one eye," Tamerlan said simply.

95

There were sounds of a scuffle behind him but before he could look, Abelmeyer attacked with twice the fury he'd had before, blow after blow barely deflected by Tamerlan. He was not as good of a swordsman as Abelmeyer. He was barely hanging on. He should have easily been beaten by now by even Liandari, never mind King Abelmeyer inside her skillful body.

His brow wrinkled at that thought even as he fought on. Had some of the things he'd learned while possessed by the Legends rubbed off. Did he possess their skills now, if only he tried to use them?

Ridiculous! You couldn't possibly have our skills!

Then why did Lila sound so desperate to deflect him?

He threw himself into the fight, trying to relax and let his arms work easily instead of controlling every motion – if he really had these skills then this should be like walking – something he could do better if he wasn't thinking too hard about every muscle movement.

Etienne fell to the ground with a pained cry his sword clattering off the ground. Who was he fighting with? Tamerlan was the one battling Liandari – or rather, Abelmeyer.

There was no time to look. The city dropped suddenly beneath him and the strong sensation of falling made his belly tumble while at the same time his feet were still on the ground.

The sound of ground smashing into ground – almost more a feeling than a sound crashed through him. Dust and ash and bits of debris formed sudden clouds over everything at the same moment that Tamerlan's bones seemed to shudder and scream in pain as they struck the earth. The dragon had landed – but only for a moment and then the ground shifted and Tamerlan could feel them lifting from the ground again.

Either something had hurt the dragon, or it had landed for a brief second and when it did, the whole city shuddered and broke again. Tamerlan swallowed down bile – trying desperately not to think about how vulnerable they were – like gnats on the back of a dog. Every shake, every leap, every roll, a chance for them to die. And the dog didn't even know.

Liandari cursed and pulled herself up from the dust. Tamerlan swallowed and then scrambled for his sword. When had he lost it? If he didn't get it right away, she'd skewer him!

There! A coating of dust covered its shimmering blade. He stumbled up to his feet, sword immediately raised in a guard position, but she was gone, rushing off into the smoke and darkness loosing a stream of curses.

Confused, Tamerlan turned to Etienne but the other man was on his knees, mouth wide open, staring in the distance. When Tamerlan turned to look at what he was staring at, he felt his mouth go dry, too.

DRAGON. Ram's voice was clear and guttural in his mind – filled with the rage of ages of hate.

Mountains. There were mountains all around them as the dragon H'yi banked to the side, letting them see the entire range below and in the bright, crystal-sharp air around them, Tamerlan could see the entire range of mountains all tangled up in one another. His jaw felt like it might drop, too.

No.

DRAGON.

And now Ram's voice carried as much excitement as hate – like a hunter with his prey walking into sight.

The entire range of mountains were dragons. Not just one dragon like the ones that slept under each city of the Dragonblood Plains, but hundreds of dragons, one on top of another on top of another, curling and twisting around each other so that where one dragon began and the other left off was a mystery. He'd seen a mirror like that in the Lord Mythos' palace – the frame had been tangled dragons with wolfish grins on their faces. These dragons were not grinning. They were sleeping. And there were so many more than the ones carved around the mirror.

Tamerlan felt like he couldn't breathe. Like a single indrawn breath might wake them all and their eyes – bigger than a human palace – would open and stare at his soul.

H'yi finished banking and this time when he landed, Tamerlan was ready, bracing himself as the city shuddered, groaned and then was still.

He gasped in the sudden silence. His breath coming in ragged spurts as if his lungs knew they might be his last.

They had landed between the mountains of dragons. And from what he could tell, they were staying here – for now at least. One dragon in the midst of hundreds. And a few small, edible humans huddled on his back.

DRAGON. DRAGON. DRAGON.

Ram the Hunter, dragonslayer, Legend-trapper was going insane in his head. As if Tamerlan wasn't already mad enough for the both of them.

DRAGON. DRAGON. DRAGON.

His chant was like a booming drum leaving Tamerlan gasping, reeling, clutching his head in pain even as his legs urged him to run – but not away from the dragons – toward them.

Fight! We must destroy them before they destroy the entire world!

Ram was insane. Utterly insane. Tamerlan spun, trying to find Marielle in the shimmering light of the moon catching on the dust in the air. She was there behind him, staring up at the moon, her arms locked around Rajit as if she had just pinned him in a guard-style hold before the dragon touched down.

Both the Harbingers were gone – vanished in the commotion. They hadn't saved Anglarok. They hadn't stopped Abelmeyer.

He gritted his teeth in frustration. The Harbingers would be back – and it would be worse because now they'd tested them and knew exactly what they were facing.

"H'yi has landed," Etienne gasped from beside Tamerlan. "This might be our one chance to get off his back and flee this city."

"Into the mountains?" Tamerlan asked. "With no supplies? No map? No idea where we are?"

"Better than dying in a city with no food, very little water and no way to escape - except this one." Etienne's eyes were bold and certain.

Tamerlan swallowed. "What about Jhinn? I can't just leave him here. He rescued me again and again when no one else would."

"I'm not leaving this city - not here in these icy mountains," Rajit said.

"You'll go where we take you." Etienne's words were cutting. He was already issuing orders. "Marielle, you'll Scent out what supplies you can. You have two hours to find us what we need."

But Tamerlan's mind wasn't on supplies or a journey through the mountains. His mind was on Jhinn. How would he get the boy out of this city without leaving the water? He couldn't abandon him here, and if this was their only chance to leave, then he had to take it - but not without his friend. Betrayal was no way to repay loyalty. Cruel indifference no way to thank a heart of kindness.

"Could you smell out a winery?" he asked Marielle gently.

"What?" she seemed surprised by his question, but she stopped listening to Etienne's list of required supplies to hear him out.

"A winery would have carts that hold barrels - and it would have barrels. I think that if I split barrels lengthwise and strapped them together and then coated the seams with pitch, that I could place all of that in a large cart and fill it with water and I could float Jhinn's gondola from the puddle he's stuck in to the cart and then he could be pulled out of the city."

"To where?" Ettiene asked aghast. "Even if you managed to get him out of the city - down cobbled roads and maybe even downhill, it would still be nearly impossible to pull a cart with all that weight. We have no oxen. We have no horses. We could maybe - the four of us - pull it out of the city, but we would be vulnerable from attack by the Harbingers the whole time, and on top of that, when we got him out of the city what would we do? We will struggle to *walk* through the mountains, never mind pull a heavy cart. And what if the water leaks? What if it drains away? Your pitch job will be fast and dirty. It won't be reliable. A rig like that - it's a very long shot. It's not worth your time or risking all of our lives. Sometimes a sacrifice has to be made. This is one of those times."

Tamerlan felt his hands trembling again, but this time not with fear or madness. This time he was angry.

"Sacrifices need to be made?" he asked stiffly. "Like when you tried to sacrifice Marielle?"

"Are you ever going to stop throwing that at me?"

"I don't know - are you ever going to stop trying to sacrifice my friends?" Even to his own ears, his voice sounded petulant. He fought to control it and his next words came out as a growl. "They aren't mountains, Etienne. They're dragons. None of us stands a chance clambering around on the peaks of dragons. And you're right, Jhinn might not survive the journey. But I'll die before I abandon a friend. Even if that means added risk. Even if that means impossible tasks to perform. Look up at the mountains, Etienne. Look at how they sparkle in the moonlight, at the skiffs of snow coating their scales. Even still,

101

you can see that they live beneath that shimmering veil. They are only waiting to wake and destroy us all."

Etienne shivered, his gaze sliding across the dragons sleeping forms just past the city. If anyone knew what power those dragons held, it was him.

It is us. Ram said. *It is the Legends who know. Each made a sacrifice to save their people.*

Which begged the question - why were they so intent on letting the dragons loose now. What changed?

None of them expected the Grandfather to kill their avatars. None of them expected that they wouldn' t come back again. Sacrifice is one thing. Sacrifice for nothing? You've tasted that. Tell me, would you do it again?

Would you?

Ram was silent. Maybe that meant 'no.'

It means yes. I won't just do it again, I'll do it again and again until the end of time. And I will use whoever I must to chain the dragons and bind them in place - just like I did then. I will use you. I will use that girl you love. I will use the dark-eyed boy of the plains. I will use anyone and everyone to keep them chained to this earth.

Tamerlan swallowed. Ram was insane. Everyone knew that. Tamerlan never should have expected anything else.

"I'll take you to the closest winery," Marielle said, dragging Rajit over to Tamerlan. "But then I'm going to help Etienne. He's right. We'll need supplies if we're going to survive those mountains. And staying here is not a good choice."

102

11: THE ROAD TO ICE

MARIELLE

The smell of urgency rolled off Etienne in crashing waves of intensity as Marielle led him through the city.

"He's mad to try it. Mad!" Etienne said, irritated beyond reason by Tamerlan.

"He's being a good friend," Marielle said, not for the first time. "He's being the person who got us this far."

She was still wincing from the devastated look Tamerlan had given her when she told him she was going with Etienne.

"I don't like you out of my sight," he'd said, so earnestly that his lower lip trembled. "I want to keep you safe."

"I understand that," she'd said, trying to be gentle. "But Etienne is right. We need supplies. And he needs my nose to find them."

"Please don't go."

"I must."

The look in his eyes of longing mixed with guilt and responsibility had almost gutted her. But she was right. They needed to be practical about this and as heart-warming as his loyalty to his friend was, they would all die if they went into the mountains without basic supplies.

"That's my point," Etienne said with a dark glare. "The person who got us here is a problem. He's the one who loosed a dragon to save a girl he barely knew. He's the one who brought the Legends back to save her again. He thinks with his heart and not with his head and that's a problem. You're not a fool, Marielle. I know you. You understand why we have to think this through, why we can't let mere emotions rule us in something this important. We need a real plan to deal with the Retribution. A real plan to get through the mountains. A real plan to save the five cities."

"I wish the dragon had landed back on the plains," Marielle said. "It makes me nervous that he's set down here. Do you think he can wake the other dragons?"

"I don't know," Etienne's scent was laced with anxiety, his eyes wild when they caught the moonlight. "What's keeping them bound to the earth? That's my question. Who is doing the rituals? Who is walking the mandalas? It makes my neck itch, Marielle. I don't like it."

"I don't like it either, Etienne," Marielle agreed. She was always surprised by how much the two of them agreed. They both wanted the cities to be back to peace and order and they both agreed it should be done practically. "And I'm worried about what the Legends want from both of you. Worried even more that they can still speak to you in your minds. That shouldn't be happening. Not without you opening the Bridge. I swear that they're trying to take control of Tamerlan by force."

Etienne looked uncomfortable at that.

"And don't tell me that your shaking hands are from nerves, Lord Mythos. You're fighting off the Grandfather. I know what a nasty piece of work he is."

"Marielle," Etienne said suddenly, steering her gently into a wall and planting on hand beside her face so he could lean in close. For the first time in a long time, he smelled entirely of himself – rust and mandarin oranges. It felt a little too intimate to scent him in this position and Marielle's cheeks heated in response but either he didn't feel the same way, or it didn't bother him. "You know that I won't let him take me over or be swayed by his charms. Please tell me that you understand that."

Marielle nodded. His closeness made her heart race - it was both threatening and oddly inviting.

He chuckled. "I can never seem to work with Tamerlan like I can with you, Marielle. He only sees me as a villain of every drama, but I know that you know the truth - that I've only ever wanted to serve my people in whatever way I must."

"I know," Marielle breathed.

"I asked you before for your help - to pledge your lot with me."

"And I gave it to you."

"I'm asking again. Help me stop the Legends. Help me quell the dragons. Help me save my people."

"I will, Etienne. I want what you want."

He sighed, as if suddenly relieved and she let out her breath, too.

There was a scream in the distance and Marielle nearly dropped the sack of things in her hands. They'd gathered a sack each of dried foods, flints, knives, a tent, and warm blankets that they'd salvaged over the last two hours and they were making their way back toward the square where Jhinn had been left.

"That wasn't Jhinn?" Marielle said quickly, but she knew it couldn't be. It was in the wrong direction.

Etienne was already shaking his head. "One of the Retribution?"

"It didn't sound familiar," Marielle breathed. "I don't like fighting them."

"Of course not. But it's not them. It's the Legends controlling them."

Marielle swallowed. "When the Grandfather took you over did you see what he saw and feel what he felt?"

Etienne didn't answer.

"I thought so," she said. "So, it *is* them we are harming. And they are trapped in their own bodies with no way to stop themselves."

His mouth had formed a hard line. "I think we should go back to Jhinn. We've found what we could."

"I think we need to find out who was screaming," Marielle whispered back. "I'm worried it was Tamerlan or Rajit."

They'd left the traitor with him. Tamerlan had insisted, saying that bringing him with Marielle was too big a risk - he might give her away. And besides, Tamerlan could build faster with a second set of hands. Marielle had been reluctant to agree. The boy was untrustworthy. And it made her nervous how many risks Tamerlan was willing to take to save her from even the slightest harm - how many sacrifices he would make for her. Sometimes it seemed he would let the world burn to keep her from being singed.

Etienne nodded, pulling away from where he'd trapped her against the wall.

"It's probably best to investigate."

They slid through the shadows toward where the scream had come from. This part of the Spice District made Marielle nervous. The shops were pushed closely together with large signs hanging over the street. There seemed to be a thousand places someone might spring out from and in the spooky silence, the nearly empty city felt haunted by the ghosts of those who had once lived there.

"What do you think the Harbingers will do if they find any other people living in the city?" she whispered as they stalked through the shadows side by side. She'd drawn her blade, but it felt like little protection against the night. The wind was at her back, blowing the lingering scents of spices past her - cardamom and cinnamon, ginger and turmeric. But with the wind at her back and the spice in her nose, she couldn't smell what was ahead and it made her feel doubly blind.

"The Legends, you mean?" Etienne asked. "They'll do what Legends always do. Use them, somehow."

"How could they use them?" Marielle asked as she turned a corner, but then she froze as they looked out across an open square, flooded by silver moonlight. In the very center, there had once been a fountain where water spurted out of a carved tree. Now, something else hung from the tree. Something that was dripping in a city without water.

"Dragon's spit!" she breathed as Etienne sank into an immediate ready-position – his blade out and his feet spread wide.

She ran to the center of the square, dropping her sack outside the fountain as Etienne cursed at her to stop. But she could smell it now – blood, so much blood and fear in the air. The fear was fresh and she didn't smell death yet. The man hanging from the tree by one foot wasn't fighting. He was neither old nor young, though he was gaunt, and his lips chapped and dry. His clothing smelled lived-in. Perhaps he had been a beggar before the fires tore through H'yi. Perhaps he hadn't left. Perhaps he had been as startled as they were when the city rose up on the wings of the dragon and flew.

But he was probably more surprised when one of the Legends caught him. And she could smell the stunned horror sweeping through him even now. Elderberry hung in the air like a mist, but whether that was from the insanity of the Legends or because the man had been mad before their arrival – she didn't know.

What she did know was that they took his eye.

The other one was glazed over and bloodshot. From his neck, blood still dripped from a ragged tear and as she tugged at his bindings, he breathed a last bubbling breath and then the stink of death overwhelmed the smells of madness and fear. She was too late.

"You can't save him," Etienne said breathlessly. He'd caught up with her. "Why did you try? You only made yourself a target."

She nodded, agreeing with his assessment even as she knew she could never *not* try.

"What did they write on the fountain wall?" she asked, pointing to where he stood on words written in blood.

He leapt down from the wall and read aloud. "'The one-eyed king sends warning. Surrender or die.' Well, that's promising."

"Tamerlan," she breathed, her heart suddenly seizing inside her. What if they attacked him like this? What if that traitor Rajit turned on him and they strung him up, too? What if –

Her feet were already moving. She had enough control to stop and scoop up the sack she'd found, but then she was sprinting down the empty streets, no longer looking at the shadows or wondering about hauntings as she dashed toward the square where Jhinn was waiting.

109

What if she found him dead, too? What if –

She could hear Etienne cursing again as he followed. He was likely sorry that she was his only ally. Sorry that she led with her heart sometimes, even though her mind often thought like his did.

But she couldn't help it. She kept seeing mental images of Tamerlan, hanging by a foot, his neck a ragged line of bubbling blood. Of Tamerlan dead, burned in a fire. Of Tamerlan with a knife in his back and Rajit standing over his body. She shouldn't have left him with that traitor – even if it seemed practical, even if he asked her to. She should have done what he asked and stayed with him even if it was for his safety and not for hers.

She'd worked herself into a near panic by the time she turned the last corner and stumbled out, gasping and heaving, into the square where Jhinn sat in a gondola in the center of the still water.

He came to his feet the moment she arrived, face drawn with lines of anxiety and smoked paprika tinged his usual strawberry scent.

"Marielle?" his voice was carefully controlled but she could smell the near-terror behind his words. "Where is Tamerlan? I heard screaming."

"Not Tamerlan," she gasped between breaths, but her eyes were scanning the three other streets leading to the square. Where was he? He should be here by now – they'd told him an hour and it had been at least two. Maybe the Legends had found him. Or, more likely maybe he'd refused to give up his project making that barrel-cart thing when it became clear that he couldn't possibly make it in just one hour.

"Does he live?" Jhinn asked, his breath hanging in the air like a wispy white flag.

"We had to separate. We were gathering supplies to leave the city now that the dragon has landed," Etienne said, coming up from behind her once again.

Jhinn's eyes went hard. A look Marielle had seen too many times. The ache in her belly wasn't new, either. Would it ever get easier to watch the hope drain out of someone's eyes?

"In the mountains," Jhinn stated. "In a place with no water."

"Not that we know of," Etienne agreed. At least he wasn't a liar. He never really had been. The nice thing about being someone who always faced reality head-on was that they never tried to pretend hope to you where there was none.

And yet Marielle couldn't help herself. She couldn't help trying to make the blow land a little lighter.

"Tamerlan had a plan for you. He was trying to make it work."

In the distance, she heard a faint sound. She was trying to concentrate on it, trying to figure out where it was coming from as she gripped her sword tighter. What were the Legends doing now? But it was hard to hear over Etienne.

He made an irritated sound in the back of his throat. "You don't help him with false hope, Marielle. And Tamerlan's hairbrained scheme is even worse. A stupid, stupid idea meant

111

to propagate a lie. Jhinn, listen to me. Your people had traditions and beliefs. That's fine. But at some point, you have to decide whether you can die for those beliefs or whether you need to abandon them. You've chosen to die. There's honor in that. But don't let's pretend it can be anything else. There aren't going to be any miracles here. I respect your people and your choice. I won't lie to you."

The sound was louder, a rumbling now, and growing closer and then suddenly a dark shape emerged from the street opposite to them.

Marielle leapt up onto Jhinn's carefully dammed wall, straining her eyes in the darkness as the moonlight picked out three shapes. It took her a moment to realize what she was seeing.

He'd done it! Tamerlan and Rajit were bent over as they threw themselves against the harnesses that should have held oxen or thick draft horses, pulling with all their might against a wine cart. And in the cart, the silhouettes of hacked and modified barrels protruded.

"Tamerlan," she breathed. She hadn't realized how much tension she was holding in until he came into sight – alive and whole, still. And under his own rule. If the Legends had him, she doubted they'd be letting him modify wine carts.

"Rajit?" Jhinn's voice sounded haunted. He fell to the floor of his gondola, the scent of shock permeating the air all around him. "Rajit, do you still roam the lands of the dead?"

Rajit froze and the cart nearly plowed into him as Tamerlan cried a warning and then shoved him out of the harness and out of the way of the cart's momentum just in time. He slowed it to a halt and then ran back for the boy, helping him back to his feet.

Beside Marielle, in the gondola on the small pond, Jhinn shook like a leaf, his lower lip trembling like he might cry and his arms wrapping around his body as if to hold himself together.

"Brother?" he asked, and his tone was so plaintive that Marielle felt herself holding her breath, waiting for the response. "Is it really you?"

Tamerlan brought a stumbling Rajit to the edge of the make-shift pond. He wasn't hurt. Just sweaty and tired. Marielle noted where a new streak of dirt spanned his forehead and how he heaved and gasped as he tried to catch his breath from the exertion of pulling the cart. He was steadying the little traitor with one hand, helping him toward Jhinn.

Rajit, on the other hand, looked like he was struck with guilt, his face pale as the moon above. His Adam's apple bobbed again and again as he swallowed and it was long moments before he was able to speak.

"It's me. I thought … I wondered if it was you, they were talking about. I didn't know anyone else stupid enough to sit in a boat in a ruined city and refuse to leave it." The bitterness in his voice as thick as the smell of it in Marielle's nostrils.

"It's like a dream come true to see you again," Jhinns tone was breathy. "I'd hoped – I'd longed for you to be – "

"For me to be what? Not dead?" Rajit's tone was poisonous, and Marielle flinched from it. She glanced to Tamerlan's face

113

and swallowed as she saw a dark expression spreading over it like a cloud. "Not penniless and abandoned by my family?"

"You were the one who was a heretic," Jhinn said quietly. "I didn't ask for that. I did everything I could to get you to safety – to give you what life I could – even if it was a shadow life in the lands of the dead."

Rajit snorted. "I'm as alive as you and those other precious idiots who won't leave their beloved water. Not even when it means their sure death."

His mouth twisted and he reached for one of the logs in Jhinn's makeshift dam, grabbing it and pulling before anyone could react. Marielle heard the gush of water at the same time that Jhinn yelled, falling off the boat and into the water in his haste to fix his dam, his heavy fur cloak pulling at him as he tried to swim.

Tamerlan leapt at Rajit with a roar, physically lifting Rajit and hurling him away from the pond. He shoved the broken piece back into the dam, frantically pushing the mud and debris back into place at the same time that Jhinn worked from the other side.

"The cart, Marielle!" he called.

What did he mean? She felt her brow furrowing, but Etienne, with an irritated sound huffing from his lips, was already on it. He sprinted around the top of the dam to the cart. Marielle chased after him, careful not to fall in the water as she balanced along the top of the dam. She joined him at the harness of the cart, shoving all her weight and strength into it as Etienne grunted beside her. It took rocking it three times to get it in motion, but then it was rolling slowly forward as Tamerlan called to them.

"Buckets! There are buckets hanging from the side!"

There were buckets just as he said.

Marielle grabbed one, tossing it to Tamerlan and he dipped put it under the crack in the dam, catching the water as it sloshed out of the pool.

"Another!"

Etienne already had the other one, trading it for Tamerlan's as Tamerlan switched buckets, handing Etienne the full one. With a filthy curse, Etienne poured the water into the barrels and traded buckets with Tamerlan.

The barrels held the water. Tamerlan had made them into something that most resembled a tank for water, though it was clearly made from pieces of barrel nailed into a framework of wooden shafts and boards and cross-members and then tarred all over with pitch.

"Will it hold?" she asked in wonder.

"It has to," Tamerlan said.

In the water, Jhinn was pulling himself back into the gondola, shivering as he took off the fur cloak and stripped out of his soaking clothing.

"We have dry blankets. Wool ones," Marielle said hurriedly, running to where she'd dropped her sack and pulling one out to give to Jhinn. "You need to put this on immediately. The cold can kill you."

"Thank you, Marielle," he said through chattering teeth.

"A waste," Rajit said like a curse. "They make a tank to transport you like you're some kind of fish. And why? To play into your delusions? To feed your madness. You're a fool, Jhinn. Just like all of them. Your mother would be ashamed of you."

Jhinn's hand brushed Marielle's as he reached from the gondola to take the blanket. In the background, the *woosh woosh* of Tamerlan and Etienne filling the barrels with the escaping water continued. And she wouldn't have noticed the extra shake in Jhinn's hand or the bitter turn to his mouth or the hot tears streaking his cheeks if she hadn't been close enough to him to distinguish between the water of the pool and the water of his sorrow.

"Waverunners," Rajit spat. "The whole lot of you are a disgrace. An embarrassment. A living tragedy. There's nothing magical about water. There's no special life to it. It's just an anchor around your neck and now you're using it to sink all your allies with you."

"We'll have it full soon," Etienne said quietly to Tamerlan. "And then we leave. Immediately. While we still can."

"Of course," Tamerlan said, a little numbly.

Marielle felt numb, too. Rajit's accusations stung. Jhinn had given everything he had to help them. Hearing him insulted like that by someone he clearly loved – seeing emotion in him when he so rarely showed it — it hurt as bad as a wound to herself.

"I'm done with you all!" Rajit yelled.

"Good," Marielle said quietly and around her they all froze, their gazes going to her face. She ignored the rest of them and looked directly at Rajit. "Because we are done with you, too. You betrayed us to our enemies and nearly lost us our lives. And now you are insulting our ally. Go. And hope the Retribution doesn't find you."

Guilt seared through her at her harsh pronouncement, but also a kind of thrill — the kind you get when you know you did a good thing in a bold way. The kind of thrill of finally doing something just in a world full of compromises, of standing on a principle in a world full of cowards. She'd do it again if she had to. And by the silence surrounding her, she thought that maybe the rest of them agreed.

Rajit scrambled to his feet and fled into the night.

12: Too Late

TAMERLAN

He was proud of her.

Of course, Marielle had stood up for Jhinn and put Rajit in his place. Her thirst to treat people with justice just made her dearer to him – more precious for her rareness. He kept scooping water, but a small smile was spreading on his face while he worked. They were close to being done filling the makeshift tank. He was going to have succeeded.

"Thank you," Jhinn said quietly. "Thank you all."

"For the record," Etienne said quietly as he worked. "I agree with your brother. But he's also a liability. He turned on us once and he can turn on us again."

Jhinn nodded. And Tamerlan felt his smile fading at the pain in the boy's face.

A ragged scream in the darkness made them all freeze for a moment. A moment later Etienne was working twice as hard as if trying to make up for his momentary freeze.

"They've found someone else. This can't go on," Marielle breathed. "It's impossible to stay here while they are out murdering innocents."

"Murdering?" Tamerlan asked.

"Liandari has been leaving trophies around the city for us to find – people that Abelmeyer has found still alive in the city – or at least alive until he catches them."

"We can't hunt them down, Marielle. We have to go," Etienne said. "Now. While the dragon is on the ground and there is time. If I had my way, we'd already be gone."

She was nodding, but her eyes were fixed on the direction where she'd heard the screams. Tamerlan felt a cold stab of ice go through him. She would always be a watch officer inside – dedicated to saving other people, to doing what was just, to saving the world. How could he keep someone like that safe when their first instinct was to run toward screams rather than away from them?

She's right. The Legends must be stopped – not killed, no. But stopped. Trapped. Imprisoned.

Don't listen to Ram. This time it was Lila again. *You don't need to stop them. But you can save your friends. Smoke and let me help you. I know a way out of the mountains. A way by water. We can bring your friend on his little boat.*

Tamerlan gasped. Was that true?

She's lying, Ram said. *She's never been to these mountains. I have.*

I can read a map, Nameless One. I know where the rivers lie – and how close we are to one.

· *She only wants her freedom and she sees you as a way to gain it forever.*

I won't use the boy – not the way you used me. Not the way you used all of us.

"Shut up! All of you shut up!" Tamerlan growled. He missed Byron Bronzebow. At least he'd been reasonable.

Reasonable? A starry-eyed idealist with no understanding of reality. Yes, I can see why you miss him. You're one and the same.

Marielle and Etienne were staring at him with concern in their eyes. Had he yelled out loud? He laughed nervously.

"Is something funny?" Etienne asked cynically. "Would you like to share the joke?"

Tamerlan swallowed. "I think we need to get out of the city as fast as we can."

The ground rumbled beneath him.

"Agreed," Etienne said.

Tamerlan reached for the gondola. "Now, Jhinn, we'll try to float your gondola directly from the pond to –"

His words cut off as the ground beneath them heaved and then lifted and his belly sank like a stone against the sudden upward pressure.

Etienne screamed a curse, "Dragon's spit!" His face was dark as he turned to Tamerlan and hissed. "Legends take your soul,

120

Alchemist! We're too late! We could have been free but we're *too late!*"

The dragon under them rose into the air, a cloud that had been in the sky above them only moments before settled into the streets, filling the night with sudden mist, distant screams, and the ragged sounds of Etienne's foul curses.

Tamerlan's mouth went dry.

You should have listened, Lila taunted. *But I suppose I don't mind. Now maybe you'll let me loose. I can bring down King Abelmeyer the One-Eyed and The Lady Sacrifice before we land again. Smoke, pretty boy! Smoke and let me make all your dreams come true.*

Even the nightmares?

They won't feel like nightmares when you're with me.

He was knocked backward against the dam before he realized what was happening, blinking in the moonlight as a pair of hands grabbed his coat and drove him against the make-shift wall around the fountain.

"I should have realized months ago what I had to do to you," Etienne said coldly. There was a rasping sound and a dagger appeared in his hand, glinting in the moonlight. "I should have realized that at the beginning of every end was you. At the start of every disaster, that was where you were. If we get rid of you, then maybe this will all finally end. The Legends. The dragons. The events that ended everything I ever loved and swore to protect."

"That's quite the speech," Tamerlan said, swallowing down fear as he tried to be clever enough to save his own life. He would like to think this was the Grandfather taking over Etienne, but he knew the other man too well by now. He saw Tamerlan as a threat all on his own with no need of anyone else's help.

"True, every word of it," Etienne said. "More than true. As the Lord Mythos, ruler of Jingen, I pronounce sentence on you – "

"No!" Marielle shouted, darting to Tamerlan's side and shoving herself between them. "Stop, Etienne! Think about this. You need Tamerlan. I need Tamerlan. Anglarok and Liandari are out there somewhere and they are killing people and waiting to kill us. And the dragon is flying again. What do we need? We need to get this dragon back down and then we need to trap it again. We need to either defeat or trap Anglarok and Liandari. Last time, they got to us first. We need people who can fight. We need people who understand at least something about the Legends and the dragons and we can't have you killing one of the only ones who do."

It sounded so logical and well thought out – and so cold. Was he only a tool to her? Only a means to an end? Did she encourage him and work with him only because she needed him like she thought Etienne did?

He watched her with his single eye, his heart breaking a little at her words. A tool. An ally. That's what he was to her.

And yet, he should be glad. He wanted her to stay away. He wanted her to be safe and that meant to be far from him. So why did it sting so much to think of her doing the very thing he desired?

Because you don't desire it, you pretty fool.

"I think we should leave Tamerlan here," Marielle said.

A little stab of pain shot through him. She wanted to go somewhere and to go without him. He wasn't sure if he was more worried that she would get into trouble without him there to help her or more hurt at her rejection. It stung like a slap across the face.

She was still speaking to Etienne. "You and I will go and hunt Anglarok and Liandari. We'll trap them ... or ... or whatever we have to do. And we'll leave Jhinn and Tamerlan here and Tamerlan can read that book and figure out what the Legends want."

Freedom, Lila whispered.

"Why the ones holding Anglarok and Liandari are so set against us. What Ram did to capture the dragons in the first place, and how we can use that to trap them, too." Marielle concluded.

Etienne was nodding. He shoved himself backward, away from Tamerlan and stalked into the night.

"Read the book. Find the answer," Marielle said, her hand brushing against Tamerlan as she drew back, too. He felt a burst of excitement at her touch followed by a stab of disappointment as he remembered that she didn't share his feelings.

123

She was gone before his dry mouth could form the words to ask her to be careful. If she died out there – if she was hurt –

He cursed into the darkness, reaching for the book. They were right. He had to find the answers before they just kept on running blind forever.

"She cares about you," Jhinn said through chattering teeth, but his words were hollow. It was Marielle Tamerlan was longing to hear them from, not Jhinn.

"We'll make a fire," Tamerlan said. "I'll find a brazier to warm you and sit with you in the gondola so I can use the light to read. How does that sound?"

"Sounds like a good way to survive the cold," Jhinn said through chattering teeth.

Well, he had a purpose. A purpose and a broken heart. He'd just have to let that pain propel him to do what he had to do so that all of them could survive.

13: What the Histories Say

TAMERLAN

By the time Tamerlan set the brazier up and built a large enough fire that it had burned down to strong embers, and by the time he'd gathered enough wood to keep feeding it, two hours had passed. He placed the brazier and piled the wood carefully in the gondola.

Jhinn was in desperate need of the warmth. He huddled in his wool blanket next to the red embers, teeth chattering uncontrollably.

Tamerlan sat on the other side letting the warmth wash over him with the bitterness of his freshly broken heart. But though he felt a stab of pain every time he thought of Marielle, he couldn't help but think of her constantly. Was she cold out there on her hunt? Did Etienne treat her with more respect than he'd treated Tamerlan? Would she smell danger before it came at her?

"She's different than you, that's all boy," Jhinn said through chattering teeth as if he could read Tamerlan's mind. "She's hard in ways that you are soft. Logical in ways that you are emotional. You just don't understand. I saw you slump after she left, but it's not like that. She has a job to do, that's all."

"What do you know of it?" Tamerlan asked roughly, but he gave the boy a smile to take the edge off.

"Just read your book," Jhinn said. Some color was coming back into his face as it warmed up.

Tamerlan brought the book out, careful with each page as he found his place.

"What does it say?" Jhinn asked.

It was complicated and long. Whoever had written the book had been very keen on flowery language and a little less keen on specifics.

"After the death of much of his party, Ram and those left with him renewed their vows of faith and penitence, and continued their climb in the mountains," he read. He frowned, skimming the pages as he summarized. "There's more here. The story of how they brought down a large wild cat that attacked in the night. The story of a huge lake with crystal shores in the mountains. A waterfall led from it and became the Alabastru river."

"That sounds nice," Jhinn sighed.

"It was a warm lake somehow – though the edges were crusted with ice – and the writer goes to pains to describe the bright blue color. Water was warm as a bath."

"Now you're just teasing me," Jhinn grunted. "Let me guess, you're imagining yourself showing this warm-as-a-bath lake to Marielle."

Tamerlan felt his face flush. "I'm just reading the book."

"Mmhmm. Keep reading."

"So, they come to a pathway of caves and this is where they get stuck. There's a great bridge here, but it's crumbling and to be able to cross it they need some kind of power. Oh yuck. Ram thinks it's a blood sacrifice, so he kills one of the young women who are on the quest with him and pours her blood over the bridge."

"Figures," Jhinn said. "Why do your kind always want to pour girls' blood over everything?"

Tamerlan paused, "You know I hate that."

The sun was coming up in the distance and the golden rays were just beginning to make tracks across the city, leaving long inky cold shadows in stripes across the ground. Here in this gondola, in this tiny pond that bobbed on the back of a circling dragon, with a brazier of warm charcoal and a small fire – it felt almost like a temporary haven against the madness.

Sacrifice. Blood for magic. Magic for blood.

As if Ram could defend such foolishness. It was indefensible.

It was foolishness. But it didn't exactly happen as described in the book. Nothing ever does.

And was he going to tell Tamerlan what really happened?

No.

Great. He'd just have to keep reading.

The book is not accurate.

Or maybe Ram just didn't want him to know what had happened.

Both things can be true at once.

"Was that really your brother – Rajit?" Tamerlan asked Jhinn gently.

Jhinn nodded. "He was a heretic. Just like my mother. Her they sunk in the water with stones chained around her feet. They were coming for him, too. My father put him in a barrel to try to change his mind – to get him to renounce his beliefs."

"What beliefs?"

"That those on the land live."

Tamerlan snorted. "You still don't believe that? Even after all of this?"

"Water is life. If you know where the life is and stick with it, then you live, too."

"And you still think that my life isn't real when I'm on the land?" Tamerlan asked.

"On the land, you've destroyed everything you love except Marielle and you're losing your mind. It doesn't look like a great life to me. It looks a lot like being walking dead."

Tamerlan snorted. Jhinn made a good point.

"Did you hear Rajit? Did you see how twisted he has become? Perhaps I didn't do what was best for him when I set him free that night. I thought that saving his life would be a good thing. Even if I was saving it for life on land."

"And it's not?"

"I *felt* better about it. Even if he lived in the lands of the dead – well, he didn't see them that way, so it seemed to me that it was good for him. But maybe I did that for myself. Maybe it wasn't good for Rajit at all. He is twisted with bitterness and anger. When I saw him – my heart leapt. It was like my dead had been returned to me. But that was not how he felt."

"Then he's the fool," Tamerlan said quietly. "He doesn't know what a good brother you are. You've been one to me when no one else wants anything to do with me."

"Only because I know what is real and I don't let illusions blind me. There's a world beyond this one – this temporary shell – and it calls to me, Tamerlan."

"And how will you reach it?"

He shrugged. "Through water. That's all I know. There's life in water."

Tamerlan turned back to the book. Jhinn thought there was a world *beyond* this one. Tamerlan thought there was a way to *save* this one.

Maybe they were both mad, but Tamerlan wasn't going to accuse Jhinn of madness when he knew he was so close to it himself.

He looked back at the book, reading again as Jhinn draped his fur cloak close to the brazier to dry it, adding a little more wood to the fire and propping up a kettle on the coals.

"So, after they bathed everything in blood, what happened?" Jhinn asked.

"It turned out there was a way across the bridge," Tamerlan said. "But whoever wrote this book doesn't seem to know what it was. He says, 'And forsooth, did not Ram the Hunter disappear into the shadows and from hence a cry came up from the belly of the earth and then the bridge did shimmer as if in sun and we walked over it safe to a man, but none dared cut down sweet Anamay in fear that to loose her spirit would loose them all.'"

"Pleasant bunch. And what was over the bridge?"

Jhinn brought two battered tin cups out of the back of his gondola hatch carefully putting tea into a small mesh holder and pouring the hot water over it. He handed Tamerlan one of the steaming cups.

"Thank you," Tamerlan said, still scanning and reading. "He talks about wonders – it's typical legend stuff. Singing swords. Caves of gemstones. Caverns of riches. Spirits. Warnings. And then this is interesting. It says, "And they lay there frozen under the mountain, their blood paying the price to lock the great serpents in place."

"That sounds promising. And then?"

"And then a chunk of pages are torn out."

Tamerlan swallowed. Whoever had torn out these pages must have realized that they contained the only important part. The part that might explain how to trap dragons. He could hear Ram laughing in his head. Maybe the Legend tore them out. Maybe that's why he knew Tamerlan couldn't find answers there.

He started reading on the next page.

"He brought magical horns down from the mountains. And metal by which he built cages. Five cages. There's the drawing of a horn and it looks a lot like the shell Marielle has – the yellow one. Hmmm."

"And?"

"And then it gets lyrical about his journey home. Down the river, meeting people, trying to bring back the wealth he gathered. And everyone asked where it came from and he told them it all it came from slain dragons."

That's true. It did.

"But not dragons he killed?" Jhinn asked. He was making small cakes in a pan with some flour he had squirreled away in a waterproof packet in the hatch in his boat. "There's not much of this flour, but I need to use it while I can."

"According to this, he was considered to have been the Slayer of Dragons, and those who were with him were treated with great respect by all the people and it was told that they captured the dragon with the help of Anamay and her sacrificial death."

"Nice lie," Jhinn snorted and then put on a fake high voice, "'Oh no, we didn't kill her for no reason, she was a sacrifice to the great dragon. Don't believe us? Take a look at these lovely riches! Maybe some can be for you.'"

"Yes, that seems to be the sum of it, but Ram seemed dark and angry to the people and when he found King Abelmeyer there was a very public dispute. It's hard to tell from the text – a lot of it seems to imply that we'd already know what it was about and the rest of it is very flowery. In the end, it seems to suggest that the King agreed to help, provided Ram trap a dragon for him. So, a criminal was led out. An old man who had been involved in an uprising of some kind. Oh, it looks like he was the founder of a cult, maybe? A group that worshiped the seasons? Or maybe that's poetic. A group that worshiped time?"

"Timekeepers?" Jhinn suggested, handing Tamerlan one of the small cakes.

He ate it hungrily, not caring that it burned the tips of his fingers and tongue. "These are good. Maybe we lucked out being trapped here in this pond."

He shared a half-hearted laugh with Jhinn and drank down the rest of the hot tea before continuing.

"Okay, so he grabs this head of the Timekeepers and they drag him up on a hill to where Ram has this cage made and they chain him inside. And Ram blows the trumpet and the dragon comes down and everyone is shocked. Ram is blowing, blowing and then it looks like magic grabs the dragons and shakes it and the old man in the cage is screaming and everyone is running in terror and then the dragon seems to be trapped in place, its eye open but the rest of it motionless and Ram grabs a girl from the crowd – or maybe they bring her to him, that part is fuzzy – and they pour her blood all over the dragon. And the dragon's eye shuts."

"I'm telling you, there has to be a better way to do things than to kill all the pretty girls," Jhinn said, sipping his own tea.

Tamerlan swallowed, looking out at the city. There was a pretty girl out there somewhere who he was very worried about. Would she stay safe? Would she be okay?

He tried to clear the lump from his throat.

"I guess the people thought so, too. They didn't even like this cult leader being used like this. So that night, they tried to break him out, and King Abelmeyer used his eye to put him back in the cage and he killed everyone who came close to the cage, but even that didn't quell them until Ram stood up and he promised this entrapment was only temporary and that someday their leader would return to them. That his sacrifice would buy them hundreds of years – or something, the text isn't specific on the exact measure of time – but that if they were willing to let him save them from the dragon, his sacrifice would keep the dragon bound – for now."

"Why didn't he just kill it? It was lying right there? Why not just chop its head off or rip its heart out or something?" Jhinn asked.

It wasn't so simple as that, Ram said. *We tried swords and axes. We tried magic. The most we ever managed was ripping off a single scale and opening up a wound – but that never killed the beast. They were not made of this world and they will not die in this world. The most we can hope for is to trap them – no matter how temporarily.*

"Well if that's true then what about that mountain range," Jhinn asked and Tamerlan nearly jumped. He forgot that Jhinn could see the Legends who haunted him as easily as he could hear them. "Why do those dragons look dead?"

They only sleep. What I did was replicate what was done to them. And that is why I can assure you that going there will not help you. Trying to kill the dragons will not help you.

Then why was he always screaming about killing dragons?

Oh, I want it. Make no mistake. I want it like I want to breathe. It consumes me this ancient desire to be rid of them and I will do anything in my power to quell them forever.

So he chanted 'Kill the dragon' when he knew they couldn't be killed?

Your mind is one long stream of thoughts of passion for that girl. Why can mine not be dedicated to a higher thing?

Tamerlan wasn't sure. This Ram speaking now seemed more articulate – less of a knuckle-dragging specter dressed in furs. Why? Had he missed something along the way? Had Ram changed – or was Tamerlan just hearing him more clearly. And why only him? Why that?

Because we are all listening, Deathless Pirate said out of nowhere. *He has never told us his story. Hearing it from your perspective is … enlightening.*

I was waiting, Ram said. *Over the centuries I was waiting for a new warrior to take my place.*

"To die?" Tamerlan asked out loud, forgetting himself, but Jhinn didn't seem to care. His gaze flicked back and forth between Tamerlan and an empty place in the gondola as if he were intently listening to a conversation.

No. To rule.

That didn't make any sense.

Read more of your book.

Tamerlan turned back to the book.

"So then the people agree that a short time of sacrifice is only fitting. So they build a city on top of the dragon and they pour a girl's blood over it again and again until they realize that they can pour it into the wound and it will keep the dragon in place for a full year and they build a clock on top of the city and put the cage into the clock to mark the time until the Grandfather's sacrifice will be over."

"Well, that makes sense," Jhinn said.

"Does it?" Tamerlan asked, his face screwed up. "It doesn't make sense of why the Grandfather can go through time. Or how the clock gave Marielle the same power. It doesn't explain why he went on a rampage to kill all the Legends when he got out."

135

"Maybe he just wanted their power."

Tamerlan shook his head. Could it be so simple?

"Or maybe he hates them. After all, they've all been trapped together for centuries. Think about how well you and Etienne get along. Imagine if you were together for hundreds of years?"

Tamerlan shivered.

"Or maybe this book only scratches the surface."

Tamerlan nodded. "Maybe it's just what the author understood. Maybe there was a lot more going on."

"So, what happened then?" Jhinn asked. He was packing away the food and putting on dry clothing and his fur cloak – dry now – as he laid out his wet clothing to dry and fed the fire again. Tamerlan was pleasantly warm but he couldn't relax. They'd heard another scream far in the distance a few minutes ago. Were Etienne and Marielle close to that? What if they needed him? Would he even know in time to help?

Would Marielle even want his help? Rejection tore through him again as fast and hard as his worry, making him swallow down a wave of humiliation. He turned again to the book.

"King Abelmeyer makes a deal with Ram the Hunter, though they don't really seem like friends. If Ram will give over the secret of how to trap the dragons, he will help Ram find another person to trap the next dragon. Together, they trap Maid Chaos."

"Let me guess, the details are foggy," Jhinn said.

"Yes," Tamerlan said with a shiver, "but I saw it with my own eyes. It was not pretty. They convinced her followers that it would give her everlasting life – but they weren't clear on the cost or how that life would be lived. They weren't clear on that with anyone."

"They all thought it would be temporary," Jhinn agreed. "None of them realized it would have to be forever. So when the Grandfather started to kill their avatars and you and the others just kept replacing them they had to realize that they weren't just trapped temporarily – they were trapped forever in the land of the dead with no way out – except through you or someone else they could grab and turn into an avatar. But that doesn't explain why Anglarok and Liandari want you dead."

"Doesn't it?" Tamerlan asked him. Because it was suddenly becoming clear to him. "King Abelmeyer still hates Ram. And I think he hopes that if Ram takes me as a true avatar, and then he kills me, that it will be the end to Ram and they can all escape."

"So all the Legends want you dead – as long as Ram gets you first. Otherwise, they want to try to use you to get a little closer, a little closer, to life again."

We never said that, Lila protested. But it was a weak lie.

"I think so," Tamerlan said tiredly.

"And Ram wants you to take his place – to keep the Legends locked in as the half-living sacrifices that hold the dragons prisoner."

"Yes."

"And what do you want?"

"I want the dragons to be gone."

Impossible. That was Ram.

"I want the cities to be saved."

Impossible.

"I want to live without blood sacrifices and Avatars."

Impossible. Impossible.

"And you can't think of a way to do that – and even if you could, they would hear your thoughts and sabotage your plan," Jhinn agreed. "Which means it can't be you to make the plan."

"What do you mean?"

"Marielle or Etienne or I will have to make the plan and enact the plan and you will have to trust us enough to do what we say when we tell you to do it or you have no hope of escaping this alive or at least with your own mind."

Tamerlan's hands were shaking as he looked at the last scrawled words in the book. They said, 'It will never be over as long as the dragons remain.'

"I don't know if I can," he said softly. "Etienne wants me dead. He thinks I'm the problem."

"We'll change his mind."

"Marielle doesn't feel the same way about me that I do about her."

"But you can trust her. She is honorable. She is good."

He nodded. She was all those things and more. She was life and happiness, safety and comfort, all rolled into one person.

"And I trust you, Jhinn," he said. "You've been a good friend to me."

"Sure, flatter me. Then ask for what you really want."

Tamerlan chuckled wryly. "I've used you and everyone else. Used you like tools. I thought it was for a good purpose. Now, I wonder if it was just for *my* purpose. I don't know if I know how to trust."

"Then you'll have to learn. Fast. Before it's too late."

14: Chase Through Bones and Ash

They'd been two steps ahead of them all night - maybe more. Every time Marielle turned a corner and found another body strung up, she knew they were doing this all wrong. They should be setting up a trap somewhere instead of chasing the Harbingers through the streets. She wasn't even certain what they were doing or why they were killing people.

"I didn't know there were so many people in the city still," Marielle gasped as they cut down another body hanging from a roof sign.

"They're the kind of people who had nowhere to go and nothing to go to," Etienne said, but she could hear the hurt behind his words. He cared about the people of the Dragonblood Plains the way a farmer cared about his animals. He felt responsible for the fact that they were being slaughtered like this for no reason. As if it were his job to protect them. She felt the same.

"It would be better to lay a trap for them," Marielle said. She felt her tattoos gingerly. Strange that the Legends hadn't used them again to call her to them. Perhaps they were biding their time, or perhaps they had merely given up that tactic.

"We have. Tamerlan and Jhinn sit in that pool like ducks on a pond. When one of them starts screaming, we'll know the Legends have descended."

"Then we should be there with crossbows and bolts or a net, or something, instead of out chasing shadows," Marielle said. She was still worried about the Windrose. Why would they give up that great tool against her? Unless they were planning something else? "This is acting foolishly rather than wisely."

Etienne laughed wryly. "It was your idea to hunt them like this. What made you want to be gone from that square so badly, anyway? Is it hard to watch your beloved going mad?"

"Who said he was my beloved?" Marielle asked, trying to seem flippant. It was hard to sound like that when all she felt was tense.

His expression when she left had broken her heart. He hadn't realized that she was doing it for him — saving him from Etienne's wrath, trying to give him time and space to read that book and find answers instead of continually giving himself for other people. But he hadn't looked grateful. He'd looked heartbroken. He hadn't taken her words to Etienne seriously, had he?

She bit her lip as she remembered it. But it was the kind of thing he might believe – Tamerlan with the sensitive heart who had been kicked again and again by the people he cared about – he would think that she didn't care just because she spoke about cold facts instead of how she felt. But maybe it was better for him like this – maybe he didn't need a distraction like her anyway. He'd given up too much to save her again and again. Maybe if she left him alone for a little while, the spell would break and he'd realize all the reasons he had to walk away, to stop saving her again and again, to go live a life with someone who didn't demand everything he had and was. Any normal man would prefer that. Any normal man wouldn't want a girl as full of drama and danger as Marielle's life had become.

She shivered.

"What if I said I can see through your pretense. I know when someone has lost their heart," Etienne said.

"Is that experience talking? Are you thinking about your Allegra?"

"She's not mine."

"She's not anyone's. But she serves your purposes, doesn't she? She sent Rajit here – and that seems to have been with the same goals you would have. She was working to take over Xin, which I'm sure you at least partially charmed her into doing."

"She needed no nudging from me."

"But perhaps she took your advice at just the right time?"

"Perhaps."

"Perhaps she came to you for advice – among other things?"

"Perhaps. There was a faint smile on his lips."

"How did that start? It wasn't like you would have seen her much when you were Lord Mythos."

He led them down a narrow alley. It was thick with darkness but Marielle smelled only ash and stone and the trail of Anglarok. There were no hidden dangers lurking here.

"I met her before then – as I told you – when I was an apprentice. We saved Xin City from the plague. And we became friends. She's ten years my senior. Ten years wiser and more wily than I am. I found her advice – helpful."

"I'm sure you did."

"Smirk all you like, but ruling is no easy task and having an outside perspective is helpful."

"Didn't your advisors mind?"

"My advisors did not know. We communicated by letter in code. Played stones by letter, but each move meant something in our own code."

"How romantic."

They exited the alley and crept through an open space where the moonlight jittered through a broken window high above. With every flap of the dragon's wings, the heavenly lights shuddered. Marielle was glad she didn't get seasick.

"It was, actually."

"That's why you sought her when your city was destroyed."

"Yes."

"Then why didn't you stay with her. Why didn't you seize power again with her?"

"That was the plan. But it was my fault you were stuck in a clock, Marielle. My responsibility to help free you."

"And now?"

"And now she might kill me as soon as take me back. Allegra is a dangerous woman."

The dragon lurched under them and Marielle caught the wall to steady herself. She fought down a wave of nausea. Maybe she did get seasick.

"If you could ally with her, despite knowing she was dangerous, can't you ally with Tamerlan?"

He clenched his jaw. "And why would I do that?"

"Because he is the key to the Legends," Marielle said. "And despite what you say, we need him to save the world. And we need him to trust us – not to fight us and destroy himself. Has it occurred to you that anything we say to him we are saying to them?"

His eyebrows rose. "Of course, I have considered that. The Grandfather raves often about that 'creeping yellow-haired spy.'"

Marielle swallowed. She knew the Grandfather hated Tamerlan, but this confirmed her fears.

"We need to make plans without him, Etienne. Outside his hearing. But we need him to trust us enough to go through with those plans anyhow."

"And what about me, Marielle. I have a Legend in my mind, too. Are you saying that I also must blindly trust you?"

She steeled herself.

"Yes," she said. "I am saying that. You'll both have to trust me."

He sighed. "You'll need a good plan. One that would be easier to make with someone trained in strategy."

"If you are such a master of strategy, then you know I'm right," Marielle said firmly.

"I find it convenient that you alone are not plagued by Legends and that somehow that means you need to have all the power." But she could tell this was only a complaint, not a real concern. He was going to listen to her. It was the only thing that made sense.

"Jhinn is also untouched."

"But he's stuck in a boat. I wouldn't call that a threat."

She snorted. "If you think he isn't a threat because he's pledged to remain on the water, then you may not be the strategist I thought you were."

He snorted. "I'll think on it. And in the meantime, you might want to talk to your boy."

"What do you mean?" she asked coolly.

He laughed. "I saw you break his heart back there. A heartbroken man will take insane risks. Maybe you should consider mending his heart – for all of us."

"I think you should stay out of it."

He snorted. "Again, Marielle, you're the one who brought me into it."

She could smell blood ahead – that and cunning. And insanity. Her heart kicked up to a faster rate immediately, all her muscles tensing.

"I think we aren't the only ones laying traps," she whispered, leaning up against the wall beside them and drawing her sword. "There is something strange up ahead."

"What do you smell?"

"Fear, tangled up with genius – which is bad. And through that run lines of blood and violence. And Legend."

Etienne tensed as they both raised their blades.

"You should try that shell," Etienne whispered. "These are not the Harbingers we are fighting but the Legends within them. Perhaps, they don't know the magic of the seas. Perhaps, you can use it against them."

She met his eyes and nodded. It was a solid idea.

She pulled the small yellow shell out of her belt pouch, letting it fit perfectly into the palm of her hand. She was sweating despite the cold, the stink of her nerves heavy in the air.

"They're just up ahead around that corner, she said confidently. "We should try to get a good look at it before we rush in."

Etienne nodded and then tilted his head toward the hulk of a burnt-out stone building beside him. Good idea.

She slipped into the empty door frame and glided silently over the charcoal that was all that was left of the floor. Thank goodness someone had made the stairs out of stone. She carefully climbed the circular staircase that ran along the outside wall. It had been set into the wall when it was built of stone. This must have been an important building at one time to garner that kind of care.

She was most of the way up the stairs when she started to hear the crying.

A child.

She knew that immediately and she was suddenly glad that Tamerlan wasn't here. Because while a child might break Marielle's heart if he was in pain, she knew it would undo Tamerlan and shred his self-control. Nothing could make him break down and smoke faster than that.

She slid her sword back into her scabbard as she reached the last stairs. She might need the extra hand if there wasn't much left of the floor. She wanted to keep the shell in her hand to use against the Legends. It was a good idea and besides that, it was the only weapon she had with any range.

She barely breathed as she silently slit up the last stairs to a small stone rim still surrounding the gaping hole where the floor had once been before it was burnt to cinders. There was enough stone around the rim of the wall to carefully inch to the nearest window and look down.

She gasped at what she saw.

They were heartless. And they were no longer the Harbingers she had known. Liandari and Anglarok had been made of honor. They'd been honor from core to cusp. They weren't kind, weren't soft, but they would never hurt the innocent or use a child to bait a trap. And they wouldn't have insulted her with such an obvious trap. Anglarok could use his own Scenting to find her if that's what he wanted. He was a prisoner in his own mind, just like Tamerlan had been.

There was no sign below of Liandari. But Anglarok was very obvious from his perch on the top of a fountain statue. The statue was of Queen Mer and he stood crouched on her shoulders, his fur cloak caked in blood and a wicked-looking sword in his hand.

What Legend had taken him over? Perhaps that would be obvious if she studied his handiwork. Was there a clue there? She tried to keep her breath even, to think this through, to use the opportunity instead of running in with her emotions high and her irrationality even higher.

Deep breaths, Marielle. Don't look at the bait. Look at the trap.

The trap was not very elegant.

He'd made a mesh of rope and wood and woven it into a make-shift net. When had he found time to do that between murders tonight?

The net hung from a rope and the rope went over a beam and tied beside him to the statue. The outer edges of the net were heavy wooden beams that would bring the whole thing down on someone and keep him there under the net – if the stone didn't crush him. If someone made it as far as the bait, all Anglarok would have to do is cut the rope and the trap would be sprung.

Simple.

Basic.

Too simple.

But even knowing that, she knew she could be trapped – and that Tamerlan definitely would be. Thank goodness he wasn't here! Thank goodness that she'd made him stay at the boat.

Because there were two cages. Two traps.

In one, a woman hung upside down, hands tied to a brick on the ground, legs tied to a heavy stone the apex of the net. Her tears ran down her forehead, dripping onto the ground and a cut ran along her side where someone had sliced her just enough to bring the scent of blood in the air – just enough to slowly bleed her drop by drop unless someone saved her.

And dangling by his feet from a heavy stone under the other net was a child, kicking and screaming and reaching for the

149

woman who was certainly his mother. Saving either one, would trap you with them. And even if you did get one down and away from the stone, you wouldn't get the other free. Anglarok would chop the rope and the stone would fall and kill him or her. And if you attacked Anglarok, he could cut both ropes and kill them both at once.

It was an impossible choice meant to make you ache no matter what choice you made. Because the only choice you could make was a wrong choice. A choice that would result in someone dying.

At least it was Etienne with her. Etienne would see this logically. Etienne wouldn't be moved by the plight of a single person when he had a world to save.

Her heart ached despite her cold logic and her eyes pricked with tears. She'd once served justice. She still wanted to. And justice would never allow this. Never.

She was going to have to stop it one way or another. But how? How did you defeat an impossible trap? How did you trap the trap-maker?

Her mind was racing so fast that she was having trouble calming it down. She took a deep breath and then another, forcing her thoughts to calm and become clear. Now was not the time for running in without thinking first.

She gathered herself together. What did she know? She couldn't shoot Anglarok off the fountain because she had no bow or other projectile and neither did Etienne.

Where was Etienne? She scanned the square and saw him nod at her from an alley on the other side of the street. She shook her head 'no' vehemently. Running in was not the solution. He needed to stay in place until she could think of one. If anyone ran in, then the mother and child would die. They had to act before she bled out, but there should still be enough time if they acted soon.

At the same time, she didn't dare let that part of the trap force her into premature action. That's why he'd done it – to make them stupid. To make them act. And if they ran in, then both of them would die. You could hope, perhaps, to leap from an alley and climb the statue to get to Anglarok, but he'd chop the ropes before you could hurt him. The square was open, and he could see all around him.

So.

What options did that leave?

Outsmarting him.

And that had to start with the Legends. Byron Bronzebow and Queen Mer were dead. Maid Chaos had a new living avatar. The new avatar that the Legends had made wasn't over the Bridge yet when Liandari and Anglarok were taken over. Etienne was still hearing the Grandfather, so it wasn't him. And Tamerlan said that Anglarok had Liandari. So – who was left?

Deathless Pirate. Lila Cherrylocks. Lady Sacrifice. Ram the Hunter.

Which of them would set up this trap? It seemed too subtle for Deathless Pirate. In the Legends, he was more of a leap-before-you-look type. She didn't know a lot about Ram except what Tamerlan had read, but she had a feeling that he would be more intent on the dragon than he was on hurting them. Which left Lila Cherrylocks and Lady Sacrifice. Lila would play a trick like this. She liked games and traps.

And yet.

There was something extremely dark about pitting the lives of mother and son against each other. Marielle felt a chill run through her. It was the kind of darkness that rejoiced when innocent girls were slaughtered on the longest day of the year. Besides, the way they were hanging – by their feet – reminded Marielle of when she had been hung upside down as they prepared to slit her throat. This felt the same.

She swallowed down bile.

This was Lady Sacrifice. She'd bet her life on it.

So, how did you outmaneuver a sacrifice? She didn't care if she died. That was kind of the point. And clearly, she didn't mind killing other people. How did you fight someone with nothing to lose?

She chewed her lip, thinking, and then gasped. There was a flurry of activity in the streets beyond the square. Her heart leapt into her throat as movement caught her eye.

No, no, no! Not now! It was too soon!

Tamerlan ran down one of the streets, sword drawn, cloak billowing behind him. She already knew without scenting him that he'd caught sight of the boy and his mother. He was going to try to free one of them. He was going to rush in like a fool and get them both killed.

Son of a Legend!

She motioned frantically to Etienne, trying to signal to him that he had to stop Tamerlan, but as he stepped out from the shadows, she saw another figure detach from the shadows, too. Liandari. Her blade was so quick that Marielle thought she'd hit him, but Etienne twisted at the last moment as if he could feel her behind him even though he couldn't possibly see her. His own sword flashed from his sheath as he met her blade for blade.

It was a double trap. It would catch them if they tried to save the victims and catch them if they waited and watched.

Marielle spat a curse but there just wasn't time to act. She was too high up to jump. There were too many stairs to get down to the square and stop Tamerlan in time, and Etienne was fighting for his life already.

Anglarok – or rather, the Lady Sacrifice – began to cackle from his place on the statue. His laughter was loud enough to drown out the whimpers of his victims.

Marielle's eyes shot to Tamerlan. She felt paralyzed like she was in a dream and she couldn't wake. There was no way to save him now.

She should have brought him with her so she could keep an eye on him.

She saw him pause and take a puff of smoke from his roll of spices.

"Dragon's spit in a cup!" Who cared if she muttered curses? It was already too late. "Dragon's blood and bones!"

If she had her way, she would suck the Legends out of every one of them. Tamerlan hadn't been lying when he said they were the enemy. They were like an echo of everything that had ever been wrong in the society of the Five Cities – an echo of past wrongs and future devastations.

Echo.

Like her shell had echo magic.

She lifted the shell, studying the swirls of turquoise and gold that seemed to flow around it. She could smell the tinge of magic coating the shell as she brought it up to her lips. Would it work when she didn't know how to use it? Could it work?

Maybe if she focused on what she was trying to do?

She needed to echo the magic that was keeping Anglarok bound to the will of the Lady Sacrifice – and though that echo, she needed to release him. If he had any shred of will left, he'd never torment citizens.

She put the shell to her lips and blew with all her might.

15: Murder

TAMERLAN

Tamerlan drew in the smoke, sucking it in with long, desperate breaths.

Yes! I told you we could help! I told you to do this! Lila's voice was triumphant.

He shouldn't be doing it. It felt like a defeat more than anything else, as if he'd given them his soul for nothing. But what other option did he have? He'd been sitting there with Jhinn as the screams grew – a child's screams and no child would suffer while Tamerlan could hear him and do something to help him. He'd been out of the boat and racing down the street with a flaming brand in one hand and a roll of spices in the other before he stopped to think or plan. If he found Marielle and Etienne there when he arrived, then he'd join them, but he couldn't count on that.

He lit the spice. But he didn't smoke it immediately – he wasn't that much of a fool. With care, he dropped the brand and drew his sword. He'd run to the screams and look before he leapt,

155

but he hadn't even reached the square when he saw the horrific trap before him.

It's genius. I couldn't build better, Lila had said. As if he cared about her dragon-forsaken traps! *Time to set us free, pretty boy. You know you can't do this on your own!*

She was crowing. This was what she'd hoped for all along. His heart was in his throat as he brought the spice up to his lips, but there was no sign of Etienne or Marielle - there was only him here. And if he had any chance of reaching Anglarok and stopping him in time, he would need supernatural speed and skill. And his only hope of that was to smoke.

Yes, oh yes! Lila cried as he brought it up to his lips and took a long drag on it.

He expected her to take him as a clash of steel against steel broke out somewhere close. Was that Marielle? Was she okay? He took another puff of smoke and began to run. But shouldn't he be possessed by now? He would have expected Lila to already have him as she laughed and leapt through the streets like a child freed from study.

I prefer to watch and wait before I act, a strangely accented voice said. *This is my first time in another's body. The experience is ... not pleasant. I do not like your smell, boy.*

Shock filled him as whatever Legend had him stretched his neck back and forth, making a cracking sound in the bones of it, as he took over Tamerlan's body. His speed increased, his muscles thrumming with power. He was focused fully on Anglarok, on getting to him before he could cut those ropes.

The Windsniffer. What is wrong with him? Has he gone mad?

Of course, he had! What did the Legend expect? He'd been taken permanently by a Legend. If that didn't make you mad, then nothing would – to live in the back of your mind with no control over your own actions – or the horrors you unleashed upon the earth.

Abomination! The Legend screamed through his mind and he would have flinched if the other man didn't have his body fully in his control.

Music, bright and wild – one long tone that reached into Tamerlan and shook him by the spine – filled the air and the Legend who had his reins seemed to smile internally.

Help has arrived. Another Windsniffer.

In front of them, Anglarok looked up at the window of a burnt-out building. For a brief second, anger shot through his eyes, but it was replaced just as suddenly by a look of relieved determination. He leapt from the statue to the ground, flinging his sword away and staring Tamerlan defiantly in the eyes.

"Quickly!" he called, his tattoos glowing brightly as if by magic. "Quickly before she returns!"

Was he asking Tamerlan to kill him? Shock rippled through him. He was no murderer to kill an unarmed man. An ally. A friend – of sorts.

You would not grant him mercy?

And then Anglarok blinked and his eyes narrowed in a bloodthirsty snarl.

157

The Legend in Tamerlan's body darted forward, plunging his sword into the Harbinger's chest so quickly that Tamerlan didn't have time to flinch or even gasp. Anglarok's eyes clouded over, slumping to the ground as Tamerlan wrenched his sword out of the other man's chest again.

Anglarok.

Tamerlan looked at him, stunned at what he'd just done.

The man had been so faithful to his cause. A worthy ally. A powerful force of good. And now he was gone – murdered by Tamerlan.

I knew this one. Anglarok of Ship White Peaks, of the Shard Islands of the Eighth Sea, a Windsniffer. I saw him on the ships of the Retribution. Let us sing the song of the dead for him.

The Legend began to sing with Tamerlan's lips as he reached down to close the other man's eyes and place a small pebble from the street on each of them. The song was low and longing – a proper dirge with hints of the salt of the sea in the very wording of it. The Legend took Anglarok's belt and pouches, wrapping it around Tamerlan's waist as he finished his dirge.

"To the salt and the mother, Windsniffer," he said dramatically. "To the water with you. The water of our tears honors you. With their salt and the blood we will spill in vengeance, we will honor you. Salt to salt. Water to water. We send you to the heart of the mother."

At least he was showing respect. Anglarok may have been a reluctant ally but he'd fought with Tamerlan to free Marielle and he deserved respect despite what he'd done at the end –

because it hadn't really been him. It had been the Lady Sacrifice.

Tamerlan felt the lie in his thoughts. Because he knew that even as the Legends controlled his body it was still him – still his body, still his fault, still his to atone for.

We applaud your sense of responsibility. The sea may not be governed, only responded to. Storms come as they may and none can stop them. They may only sail into the storm's teeth with shoulders back, head high, screaming defiance over every wave and swell!

This Legend made him think of Byron Bronzebow.

Who was he?

They sprinted toward the mother first, and the Legend had his knife out before Tamerlan could think, concentrating on the thick strands of rope holding her hands. He sawed through them, eyes completely focused, not distracted by anything. The gag went next and as she thanked him in a thready, weak voice, he balanced her in one arm while he cut the bindings to her feet.

They were vulnerable like this - both of them under the trap. He could still hear the sounds of steel striking steel and the harsh sounds of exertion as the people in the distance fought. He still didn't know who they were. Legends send it wasn't Marielle. Legends send her safe.

Why do you pray to us when you know we cannot help you?

A good question. You'd think he'd have stopped such nonsense now. And yet he called on them instinctually.

The woman was loose now, Tamerlan laid her on the cobblestones as gently as he could – outside the net of course, outside of danger. This Legend was strange, his actions so close to what Tamerlan's own would be that he kept forgetting himself – thinking it was he who worked and not his temporary master. He was already rushing toward the boy, ignoring his sobs as he slashed at the ropes at his feet and caught his small body in strong arms.

"Mother?" his voice was so clogged with tears as to be barely distinguishable but Tamerlan felt a surge of relief. He lived. And he knew where he was. That was a good sign.

Tamerlan brought him to his mother, joy welling up at the sight of their embrace. Her wound needed tending. The Legend was already reaching into Anglarok's belt pouch with sure hands and finding what he needed to tend to her as she spoke comforting – though weak – words to her boy.

"The Windsniffer's cloak can be used to warm you when you have the strength to rise," he was saying with Tamerlan's voice as he pulled needle and thread from the belt pouch. His actions were smooth and quick. Only moments had passed since they cut her down and already he was stitching with sure hands.

I was surgeon to my ship for a year as is custom on the ships. Each young officer takes a rotation at each station. This was long ago – before I was Admiral of the White Ships, but I was particularly good at it, and the training sticks.

So, he was an Admiral. On ships. Was he the Legend that Tamerlan had seen them creating in Choan?

You saw that? The Admiral seemed shocked. *We were not certain it would work. We've only done it once before — long, long ago when we bound the dragon under the city Xtexyx on the Eight Isles.*

If Tamerlan had control of his body, he would have felt his eyebrows raising. They had dragons across the sea, too?

Only one. Sort of.

That qualifier was not comforting. Was he referring to the egg that the Harbingers had drawn on the map?

The Legend's hand fumbled for the first time as he wrapped the bandage around the woman's wound. He was unsettled by Tamerlan's mention of the egg. Interesting. Maybe Anglarok and Liandari weren't meant to reveal that.

Some secrets are better left secret.

That was certainly true.

We'd best get the cloak from the dead to cover this woman before she shivers to pieces.

Beside them the woman clutched at her boy - he was maybe eight or nine. The tears flowing down both their faces intermixed with joy.

"My Pano, my sweet Pano," she was saying, rocking him and kissing his hair. A flash of memory of his own mother holding him in her embrace before he was sold flashed through Tamerlan's mind. He'd known a mother's love once.

A smile flickered across his face. He'd been right to risk everything for these two. But he shouldn't have won that

161

battle. It shouldn't have been so easy. What had brought Anglarok back to himself for those few moments? Had it been the horn cry he'd heard?

The Spirit Singer shell?

Was that what it was?

A powerful Windsniffer helped us.

Marielle? Who else could that have been? Tamerlan was too deep in thought as the Admiral turned them to notice that something wasn't right. Something hit him in the head, and he fell to the ground with a grunt. There was a guttural cry above him and he struggled, trying to twist up to see who had attacked him.

Blood, hot and thick dropped onto his cheek as something tugged his head back by the hair, baring his throat.

Admiral?

There was no response.

Admiral?

His breath was coming in quick gasps.

It's too bad he was stronger than me, pretty boy. Your last thoughts will be wishing he wasn't, Lila said. *I could have saved you.*

There was a grunt and the sound of meat being struck with a cleaver and then the hand was jerked from his hair and he spun immediately, shoving at the leg pinning his prone body to the cobblestones. He got it off and rolled out from underneath, fighting to get his feet under him as they slipped in blood.

In front of him, Anglarok was trying to stand, too, the gaping hole in his chest not deterring him at all. But he couldn't rise. A sword split into his head and then his face, and then his neck, carving into him again and again with horrific force. Blood spattered across Tamerlan as he finally found his feet, his mouth open in horror as he looked up to see Marielle's face twisted with a combination of panic and determination. She hacked at Anglarok a final time and his head rolled away down the cobbles.

Tamerlan gasped and her gaze met his. She choked and he rushed to her, worried. Was she hurt? Was she dying?

But it was only a sob bubbling out of her as her knees weakened and her sword – slick with blood – fell from her grip.

He rushed to her, catching her before she could fall and pulling her away from the carnage and into his arms.

"Anglarok," she breathed.

"It wasn't him," Tamerlan said gently, pulling off his glove so he could brush her hair from her face where it was tangled in a nest from her frantic battle. "It was a Legend. A Legend who took him back even after he was dead. You mustn't think it was your friend."

She wouldn't look at him, her face turned to the side as if ashamed to meet his gaze.

"Marielle," he tried to catch her eyes with his, making his as soft as he could, as gentle as he could. "It wasn't your friend. It was a Legend."

"I swore to him," she said in a small voice. "I swore to pursue justice with him. He didn't deserve this."

"It's not your fault."

"It *is* my fault!" Her lower lip was trembling, and it made him ache all through to see her in such pain. He wanted to kiss it all away, to draw it out of her with his embrace, soak it into him instead. Tears fell from her eyes, hot and steaming in the cold air, leaving tracks down her cheeks and lining her too-bright eyes in red. "If it wasn't for me, they never would have come here. They would have stayed in Xin, but they came looking for me because I swore to them."

"It's not your fault Marielle, it's not." He gave her his best smile even though his own heart was breaking, which felt ridiculous as he knelt in the street in the blood of a friend – as he listened to a curse that he was sure was Etienne fighting in the distance, as he listened to a weeping mother comforting her child, as his own heart broke, broke, broke for Marielle and all she'd been put through in the last months. He'd thought he was saving her when he drew her out of the clock, but he was wrong. She still needed saving. "Look at me, Marielle."

She looked at him from the corner of her eye, guilt shadowing her face. She was too ashamed to even look at him.

"Look at me," he said gently, opening his eyes wide and innocent, stroking her arms with his bare hands. There was a fleck of blood on her cheek. He wiped it away with a thumb. And in a huskier voice, he asked again. "Look at me."

She met his gaze, her bottom lip trembling, the tears still rolling accidentally from her horrified eyes.

"Don't look at anything else. Just me. Can you do that?"

"Yes." Her voice was raw and choked with tears. "I feel like I've broken my soul. And it can't ever knit back together again."

"Then let me put it back together for you," he whispered, taking her face in his hands and stroking her cheek with a thumb. "Let me patch your cracks and bind your hurts and tie you together."

She nodded as if she was afraid to speak out loud. She felt like a bird caught in the hand – hold it too lightly and it would fly away, hold it too tightly and you'd hurt it. He held her gently, but with a firmness that he hoped would tell her he wasn't going anywhere.

He leaned in close and with the most delicate touch possible, he brushed his lips to hers. It was only meant to be comforting, to show her that she was beloved, whole, beautiful – still. But her slightly desperate moan, as if his acceptance stung her raw soul broke something apart in him and instead of drawing back, he pulled her forward, wrapping his arms tightly around her and pulling her against his chest. He wanted to keep her there forever.

"I'm going to keep you safe, sweet Marielle," he whispered.

"You can't keep me safe from myself. Look what I've done."

He was already shaking his head as he took her face in his hands again and kissed her fervently – her forehead, her cheeks, her nose, her chin, and her sweet, sweet lips as he whispered.

"I understand, Marielle. I, of all people, understand. I know who was in that body of Anglarok's when you killed him. He was already gone. It was nothing but a specter left. And I know how you feel. I know what it's like to have to do things you never wanted to do. To lose yourself. To break yourself. Just don't give up on me, Marielle. Keep fighting. Because I really am going to find a way to put you together again. You're pure wholeness and goodness to me. You're life. Don't treat yourself as shameful, because you have nothing to be ashamed of. Ever."

He ended his words with another gentle kiss on her lips, closing his eyes so he could focus on trying to offer her everything he had left in that single moment – in giving her the very best of himself. Her response – joyous and enthusiastic – knocked him backward in surprise. Did she –? Was it possible that she wanted his embrace as badly as he wanted to give it? The possibility choked him up and he leaned back into her, his kiss turning passionate and deep.

If a kiss could heal, he'd heal her like this. If it could bind up wounds and mend a broken heart, she could have all his kisses. Every one. As many as she ever wanted.

His stomach seemed to drop inside him, and he felt like he was falling, but he clung to her, refusing to stop kissing her. She was the one putting him back together. She was the one righting all his wrongs.

The ground under them shuddered and with a *boom* the earth shook around them.

Earth.

Ground.

They'd landed again.

He gasped, eyes opening in shock. Marielle's wide eyes mirrored his.

"I have to get Jhinn while I can." His words tumbled out. It was the worst thing you could say after a moment like that.

"The little boy and his mother," Marielle gasped, her hands falling form him in her own haste.

They both scrambled to their feet, almost turning away from each other.

"Wait!" Tamerlan gasped. He kissed her quickly. "Don't let that be our last kiss."

And before she could answer he was sprinting down the street to help his friend.

16: Dragon's Landing

It took a moment for her to clear her head. The scent of him still filled her nose, her mind, her every pore like he was still here kissing her.

She'd never done that before – with anyone – which was why she hadn't realized that it would make his scent a thousand times stronger until it filled her to intoxication and all she wanted was more and more and more. It was worse – and better, oh so much better – than magic. It fogged her mind and made her love it fogged. It dulled every other sense and she didn't miss them for a second. She just wanted to drift forever in this intoxicating cocktail of scent and taste and touch.

She'd almost forgotten the sharp pain that sawed through her moments before it started. Almost forgot to hate herself when he kissed her hurts away.

She blinked, swallowing hard and trying to force her mind to focus again.

They had landed. And that meant they had to get off the dragon's back while they could.

She shook her head, finally finding her balance and ran to the woman and child. "You need to get out of the city as fast as you can. Can you walk?"

The woman nodded.

"We're in the mountains. You need to head east once you're out. There will be people east. If you have food or clothing stashed somewhere here, you must be quick to get it."

Her child had stopped crying, though he looked at her with huge eyes, shivering in the cold.

"Here, take my cloak," she said, wrapping the fur around him. "Bring any fuel or lanterns or warm clothing you have or can find."

"We didn't have the money to leave the city after the fire. And there were stories about what people were doing in the refugee camps," the woman said. "They treat them like cattle. There is disease."

"I understand," Marielle said. What decision would she have made? With a child? With his whole life in her hands? It was impossible to judge when she'd never had that responsibility. "But you have to hurry."

"We have things we collected. We have as much as we can carry."

"And the wound in your side? Can you walk?"

"Can we go with you?" Her eyes were desperate, but Marielle shook her head.

"We're going into deeper danger," she said quietly, looking at the range of mountains on one side of the city. The dragon had settled back in among the peaks. Perhaps he liked it here with the rest of his kind. "And we attract trouble and violence. You must get your son as far from here as you can." She swallowed. "I wish I could do more to help you."

"You've done enough," the woman said, her face hardening as she braced herself mentally for a journey through the cold with a child and limited supplies. "We will go east and find people."

Marielle nodded. "Go fast. Before the dragon rises again."

The woman took her son's hand and they hurried away, leaving Marielle standing over Anglarok's mangled corpse in perfect silence.

Silence.

That wasn't right. What had happened to Etienne?

She looked up in time to see him jogging up the street, sweat slicking his face despite the cold. A rag was tied around his left hand. She could smell the blood, coppery and raw.

"She was fast but when you slaughtered her friend her fury dulled and when the dragon landed, she slipped away," he said, shoving a fur cloak at Marielle. "This slipped from her shoulders. It looks like you'll need it."

Marielle glanced toward where the woman and her boy had fled. She needed it more than Marielle did. But they were already gone.

"Thank you." She wrapped the cloak around her. "I don't think there's time to bury Anglarok."

Etienne snorted. "Maybe this time Tamerlan will get his friend loaded up in time before the dragon rises again. We'll grab our supplies and go."

Marielle nodded. There might not be another chance to get off the dragon. And these last few minutes had shown her how pitiless the Legends would be if they were let free.

"Which way did Liandari go?" Marielle asked as they ran toward the square after Tamerlan. She hadn't stopped to catch the other woman's scent. She wasn't sure if she would have even been able to if she wanted to. Tamerlan's scent still filled her, surrounding her, intoxicating her.

"She was headed out of the city by the quickest route. North. Same as we'll head when we get our gear."

Marielle nodded. And what would she do after that? What was Abelmeyer planning to use her for? Hopefully, Tamerlan had learned something – anything – from the book.

"The shell worked. But only for a moment," she confessed as they jogged side by side.

"A moment was all that was needed. Tamerlan almost ruined our plan. That boy needs to learn to think."

Marielle shrugged. He had almost ruined it – but in the end, he'd been in the exact right place at the right time. And would she really want a friend who saw a child in danger and did nothing? Tamerlan had been willing to smoke to free him.

A thought came to her and she stumbled as she tried to freeze and run at the same time.

"Careful there!" Etienne's hand reached out to steady her.

Had that been Tamerlan kissing her and saying those sweet, life-giving things, or had that been the Legend who possessed him?

Just the possibility of that chilled her.

Would she always have to worry about whether his actions and words were his own? Would she never know what was true? A tiny blossom of doubt sprang up in what had been pure joy only moments ago.

For a brief moment, the heavy scent of him filling her nose was not as comforting as it had been.

The Legends ruined everything.

They reached the square panting and exhausted. Etienne was already grabbing the sacks they had stowed next to the dam, but most of them were missing, and even more shocking – Jhinn, the gondola, the cart, and Tamerlan were all gone. Marielle spun, looking down every street. She saw no visible signs of them but his scent trail was so thick that she could have followed that golden scent of him – the hot honey and lavender scent that made her want to breathe more and more of it in with every gulp – she could have followed that anywhere.

Etienne gestured at a muddy patch where a cart track was clearly visible in the mud.

"Smart. He pushed him downhill. Though how you'd stop a cart once it's rolling, I don't know. He won't be able to pull it once it stops, either. He must be running hard just to keep up."

Marielle followed his gaze to a down-hill path. They were close to the center of the city – but depending on how the dragon was lying and the layout of the streets, it could be possible to get as far as the city walls without having to stop. If you were very, very lucky, then you might even line up with the right street to go over a bridge and through a gate and out of the city.

"The chances of that seemed slim," she muttered. But his scent was laced with confidence and hope. Maybe he knew something she didn't. Or maybe that was just Tamerlan – always hoping, always trying, always loving despite all odds. She could still taste him on her lips and in her mind. She wanted to kiss him again, to be sure it was all real.

Etienne snorted. "I think this is a foolhardy plan of his. I am not fond of Tamerlan Zi'fen. I worry that eventually, his father will shine through. And I wonder what happened to his seven other brothers. Where are they in all this mess? Are they at home cooling their heels? And what is to stop him from joining them? He has no connection to our lands and cities. But there is one thing about him I do know."

"There's a but to all this?" Marielle said, nearly rolling her eyes as she began to jog down the road, that Tamerlan had taken. It would lead out of the city. And maybe they could catch up with him along the way.

"Yes. He's lucky. He trips over important things. He just 'finds' what he needs at the right moment. That's someone useful to have around. Just watch. We'll get out the city gate and discover him and Jhinn and that ridiculous cart of water all there and in good order."

Or they'd find it smashed to bits and Jhinn suicidal on the side of the street somewhere. That was also possible. She could smell Jhinn – barely – in the intoxicating tangle of Tamerlan's trail. Jhinn's scent tasted anxious and slightly desperate.

With worry in her heart, too, she ran.

Hopefully, the mother and son were finding their way out of the city. She patted the shell that was back in her belt pouch, watching the shadows in case Liandari popped out of them and worrying like crazy for Tamerlan and Etienne. She wouldn't be able to smell Liandari if she was lying in wait. This trail was too strong, too powerful for anything else to penetrate it.

"Are we going to go into those mountains and look for whatever Ram found?" she asked Etienne as she ran.

"You tell me. I thought you were the one with the plan that the rest of us couldn't be trusted with," he said wryly. But his words had a sadness behind them – as if he was actually admitting she was right to be worried about that.

"Do you feel hopeless, Etienne?" she asked.

"Frequently."

"Right now?"

"Absolutely."

"Then what keeps you going?"

"I'm not the kind of man who quits. Most people quit right before the solution comes. Right before they finally make good. I will not go out that way. They will find me clawing my way on my belly with bloody fingers and every nail missing before they find I quit at anything."

"I think that's better than luck," Marielle said gently.

"Tenacity is always better than luck," Etienne agreed. "Unfortunately, the alchemist has that, too."

Marielle chuckled as she ran. But at least she had Etienne trusting them again.

And there was only one Legend out hunting them now. They had to just get out of the city before the dragon launched again. Then she would try to track her way through the mountains by smell alone to find whatever it was they needed. It was a long shot – but everything about her life since Etienne hung her up and tried to slit her throat, had been a long shot.

It was an hour before they reached the edge of the city and slid through the gates in the bright afternoon sun. The sun here had a strange almost white quality that was different than the yellow-gold of the sun on the plains. A dusting of light snow blew down in icy particles from the sky, leaving rainbow-hued patterns in the air but not gathering in piles on the ground or

175

accumulating anywhere. It made the cobbles icy and slick as they stepped from them and out what had once been the gate onto the rock beyond.

There were more tracks here – skidding over the light snow on the ground and leaving wavering tracks. Which meant they were still on the trail of the run-away cart. The rock of the mountain here drifted slightly downward and Marielle could see where the cart tracks followed the incline and went around a banked curve and out of sight. The scent trail went with them, stronger somehow in the fresh air.

She scrambled along the slick rock until a hand grabbed her arm. "How long are we going to follow them for? Maybe we should decide where we are going to go from here?"

"And leave all that luck for someone else?" she asked coyly.

He snorted.

But now she was getting nervous. Unlike in the city, the snow here stayed on the ground, slowly accumulating flake by flake to blanket the earth in a light covering that hid everything she wanted to see. And the fresh, effervescent scent was so cleansing that it seemed to wash away all other smells until all she could smell was snow, snow, snow.

She could still follow Tamerlan and Jhinn's scent trails, but it worried her that they seemed to block out all other scents. What was she missing?

There were other smells she didn't recognize on the edge of her senses – strange smells she couldn't place that tickled her nose just enough that she knew they were there, but not enough to identify them. Were they walking into a trap?

They were about to turn the corner when Etienne paused, hand thrown out to make her stop, too. He drew his blade slowly, shaking his head as if he were uncertain about something.

They turned the corner and emerged in a rocky haven between the high rock walls. As the center was a small lake, glowing brightly. The cart was broken against a rock beside it, the barrels split and one of the wheels completely off the axle. But the gondola was floating along the shore of the lake and a very wet, very shaken looking Jhinn perked up the moment he saw them.

"Marielle!" He grinned at her as she came close. "We did it! Look!"

"You made it in the water without hitting the ground?" she asked, curious. She could smell Tamerlan's scent everywhere, but he wasn't in sight.

"Tamerlan is getting wood for a fire," Jhinn said hopefully as Marielle set her sacks down on the rock and looked around.

"This isn't much of a lake," she said eventually.

"It extends under a rock ledge over there, though," Jhinn said. "It's hard to see but it's a cave of sorts."

Marielle swallowed. Tamerlan had brought him this far, but with the cart ruined and this lake so small and dead, how would they ever get him out again?

177

"Thinking about what a fool you are?"

The words had an almost ringing quality as a figure climbed out to where they could see her at the top of one of the rocky cliffs surrounding the lake.

Liandari.

She wasn't done with them.

17: Cave Pictures

Tamerlan

He'd meant to go find wood. In this weather, Jhinn needed to start a fire in the brazier if he was going to keep from freezing to death.

That's what he'd meant to do.

He'd followed the line of rocks looking for wood and found a few sticks blown up against the side of the rock, but when he gathered them up it had revealed words chiseled into the rock.

If it was rock. The rock here was a little too smooth, a little too regular, a little too close to a pattern of man-sized scales to make him feel comfortable. This rock looked like the underside of a leaf turned upside-down so that you could see the delicate threading of the veins on the blade of the leaf. He'd stopped for a moment, running his palm over the leaf-like scale, completely entranced by the intricate pattern of the veins — more delicate and artful than anything he'd seen in the palaces he'd entered over the past few months, and yet carved out of rock.

Dragons, Ram said in his mind. *You should not be here. You must return to the cities. You must trap the dragons that have been freed, replace the Legends that have been killed. You must hunt as I once did.*

Hunt innocent people and bind them to eternal torment in a world between worlds? That's what Ram wanted for him?

It must be done. Even the worst of tasks must be done by someone. A servant of all. A hunter.

Tamerlan shivered, his palm pressed against the stone dragon scale. He almost dreamed he could feel warmth through it.

Can't you? The dragon is alive. It merely sleeps.

By why did it sleep? How did it sleep?

You already know how. Through the sacrifice of an avatar? What more do you need to know? Return to the Dragonblood Plains and take up my cause. Save your people.

Ignore him, Lila said, cutting into his rant. *When has Ram ever done anything for you? He's a madman. Let's go see what he's hiding.*

I hide nothing.

Lila's laugh was threaded with hate. *You hide everything, Hunter. From your victims, from this boy, from the dragons. You are nothing but secrets within secrets within secrets.*

Tamerlan shivered and his hands slipped across the snow, brushing it from words chiseled into the scale below the one he'd been studying.

TURN BACK, it read – but in the ancient runes he'd studied in his father's libraries not the language of the plains.

Well, that was welcoming. Were there more greetings in the rock?

He walked a little further along the side of the dragon, brushing snow off and collecting a few sticks as he went.

HERE BE DRAGONS, the next chiseled letters said – also in runes. The runes made him think of the old recipe that opened the Bridge of Legends. It had been in these runes. They were dark – almost as if they were stained with blood. But it had probably been centuries since they were carved.

Carved into the flesh of our enemies.

Ram was not a pleasant companion to have in his mind with him.

Pleasantness is not my aim.

Of course not. And now he was walking – almost without meaning to – into a cave mouth. And here at the mouth of the cave, someone had etched pictures into the rock. At first, as he brushed the snow away, he was confused about what they depicted, but once he saw them clearly, he wished he had not seen them at all.

Horror filled him. No human should think these things, never mind draw them – never mind take the time to chisel them into stone. One picture led into another and into another. Pictures of men and women doing unspeakable horrors to one another.

And around them tangled the tails and snouts and clawed feet of dragons. Tamerlan swallowed down bile.

There was a strange glow in the cave. It went against all his instincts to go any further. Not after the warnings. Not after the grim horror of a madman's fantasy. And certainly not with the maniacal laughter that had begun in his head.

Is not life a joke and death a greater joke? Ram asked as his laugh went on and on and on, chilling Tamerlan to the core. If he could have just one more wish, he would be free of the Legends forever.

He still didn't know whether he was insane or simply a sane man haunted by devils.

I share your sentiment, the Admiral agreed.

Tamerlan paused. He hadn't expected support, but it was washed away by another burst of Ram's insane laughter. Tamerlan swallowed. Was this his own destiny – to go mad like Ram and destroy everything dear to him?

Is it madness to know the secrets and have to live with them? Ram asked. *Is it madness to know the truth that no one else wants to see? That they would rip their own eyes out to unsee?*

There had been depictions of that, certainly.

Is that what you fear, Tamerlan? Physical horror? Then you should do as I tell you and leave this place.

Now that he was in the cave entrance, he didn't need to brush snow away to read what was carved in the wall.

Blood of heart and bone of bone,
Life and love poured out on stone,
Keep the snap and claws at bay,
All men are but made of clay.

Empty shell and dead as rock,
Open doors and turn in lock,
Death the key to all you need,
No plea or cry the hunter heed.

Laugh we who your death behold,
Dance we who in the dark are told,
Light of foot and light of heart,
As we pick over every part.

Fear not that your death be null,
Every human sees the cull,
Spirit to spirit, ash to ash,
Neck to throttle, skull to bash.

Someone had taken the time to delicately carve every line of the gruesome poem into the wall as if to lovingly keep it for generations to come. And suddenly Tamerlan wanted to listen to Ram the Hunter. Because the one thing he surely wanted to avoid was walking into that cave and seeing what the people who had thought these pictures and this poem were art might have left for someone like him.

He still wasn't over the horror of it all when a scream shredded the air and he dropped his sticks and ran toward it.

18: It Can Always Get Worse

MARIELLE

She hadn't expected Liandari. Hadn't smelled her. She was already half-cursing Tamerlan for putting her in such a trance with his unbelievably sweet smell and blinding her to all others when Liandari dragged Rajit out from behind her. He trembled in fear, seeming almost frozen by it.

"I found something of yours," she said dryly.

"Abelmeyer?" Etienne asked boldly. "Back for more?"

"No," Liandari said. She slung Rajit over her shoulder like he was no more than a sack of grain and then she leapt from the small cliff to land on the stone beside them. Marielle felt her mouth drop open. You couldn't do that - not and survive. And yet here she was, perfectly fine. She dropped Rajit beside her, but her knife was at his throat.

"I want you gone from this place," she said calmly. "You leave, or I kill the boy. He was with you. You must care whether he lives or dies."

Marielle's gaze flickered to Jhinn's face. He cared. She could see it in his desperate expression and the waves of orange scent drifting from him. He was crouched in the gondola, dripping wet, a knife in one hand as if he could do anything at all to help his brother. That would only make a difference if Liandari decided to swim for it - and Marielle didn't think she was that much of a fool.

"What do we care if you kill him?" Etienne asked. "We don't need the boy."

"Don't you?" Liandari asked with a laugh. Her voice didn't sound right. It was becoming easier to notice those things. Dignified, noble Liandari would not have spoken this way. How odd to think that she was more measured in her speech than a king. "He was with you, so I thought he might be dear to you. But if that is not the case, then you still need him."

"I think not," Etienne said, and his air of cool indifference chilled even Marielle. She could smell his scent - determined, confident. He didn't have the same feelings of guilt she did at the death of others. He wasn't troubled by fear that Abelmeyer might slay Rajit simply to spite them.

"Can you not smell the magic in the cave beyond?" Liandari asked, her gaze on Marielle.

Marielle let her nose wrinkle, trying to dispel the scent of Tamerlan as she let her senses reach out. There was magic there – vanilla and turquoise with flecks of gold. Her forehead furrowed as she tried to think. Why would there be magic beyond? And what was that other scent tickling the edges of her senses? It smelled familiar. Like magic mixed with

186

something else. Like the clock she'd been trapped in. It smelled a bit like that.

She was still frowning when Liandari continued, "What do you think happens if a Legend were to, say, jump out of a clock and leave their *real* avatar behind? Would it break the magic they sacrificed to make something? Would it free a dragon? Would it kill that body they left?"

"I suppose you must know," Etienne said coolly.

"Oh, but I don't. But I suspect it might. And I suspect that your Scenter might be wrinkling her nose because she is catching a whiff of death from the cave beyond where the Lady Sacrifice's former avatar now rots, her body no longer sealed by the magic that held it in place."

Marielle gasped. That was exactly what she was smelling. If she concentrated, she could almost pick out each of those different kinds of decay. She swallowed down bile as it rose in her mouth.

"See?" Liandari said triumphantly. "She does smell it. And so you must realize what I did. You'll need to replace that avatar now that you've killed Anglarok who housed the dear Lady Sacrifice. Which means you'll have to kill someone. And if you don't want to kill a friend, you'll need some other victim. Like maybe this one."

"We aren't going to be making a new avatar," Marielle said.

"Aren't you?" Abelmeyer taunted. "Aren't you letting the alchemist boy lead you? And he's being led by Ram the Hunter who is bound and determined to make a brand new hunter out of him. And that means new avatars. New, fresh deaths. New, horrific ways of creating them. And since you're his friends, I guess you'll be helping with that."

"No," Marielle said quietly. "I follow the law, not the whims of necessity."

"The law isn't that simple. Is there a law without a city? A law without a government?"

"There's the Real Law. The law that branches over everything else like a tree."

"We tried stopping you in the bookbindery," Abelmeyer said. "We tried to show you what we can do when we work together, but you didn't listen. So, now I'll show you. You want things back to where they were? You want to keep us trapped forever behind the Bridge of Legends? You think this is somehow serving your *real* law? Then you're going to have to kill people in horrific ways. Are you ready for that, Scenter? Ready to smell their terror? Ready to scent the violence? Let the waves of their horror and panic swell around you in clouds of colorful scents?" He paused. Or she did. Or whoever that was in that amalgamation of person. "Or maybe that's what you love? Bathing in the terror of others. Breathing it in. Letting it soak deep into your heart and bones so that you are made of their last breaths and last, broken dreams."

"No," she gasped, tears springing to her eyes and then a last powerful, "No!" as she stood up and pulled the shell from her belt pouch and blew a steady, strong note. She pushed as much as herself as she dared into that one desperate plea for echo magic. Please, oh please! Work this one time, again! Please!

188

Her nose was flooded with the lilac and vanilla smell of magic. But Liandari was already sheathing her knife and drawing her sword. She faced them with her head turned slightly to the side, as if she were compensating for a bad eye despite having two eyes that worked perfectly.

Marielle blew through the shell again. Work, work, work!

Liandari paused for a half a second and in that second Rajit leapt forward, grabbing the knife from her belt and jabbing it into her side.

She roared in pain, lifting her sword and swinging it as Etienne darted forward. He'd fought her before and beat her. He could do it again. Confidence filled his sharply chiseled face as he slashed toward her but her first blow had not been for him. A wicked slash parted Rajit's shirt and blood poured from the wound even as Marielle leapt forward, joining Etienne's defense.

He fought with a sword as quick as a viper's tongue. It flashed out toward throat or inner arm fast as light, and then it was back again, guarding its master.

"I can't let you pick up where Ram left off," Abelmeyer said through Liandari's voice.

"I can't let you stop us," Etienne returned, but she was working him hard and even Marielle's defense of his left side was not helping enough. She turned Liandari's blade aside with a quick riposte before it snaked in on his left, but the Harbinger was so fast that she was already beginning another attack before Marielle could even catch her breath.

189

Behind the daughter of Queen Mer, Rajit lay on the ground, clutching his chest and moaning. That cut had been deep. Marielle heard Jhinn calling to him.

"Hold on, Rajit! I'm coming." He might be able to reach from the gondola. Maybe.

Her thoughts were interrupted as a flurry of blows rattled her sword almost out of her hand. The last thrust was so close that she barely dodged to the side and it grazed her scalp. Blood, hot and fast, spread down her cheek shocking her with its sudden warmth. She swallowed down a sudden wave of dizziness as Etienne cried out.

"On your left!"

She barely got her sword back up to defend herself but now the blood was in her eyes and she had to blink fast to clear it enough to see. Etienne cursed loudly – he'd been struck. She could smell the wound.

"Help me get you in the boat! Please, Rajit!" Jhinn was calling and Marielle blinked hard. She felt disoriented in the chaos of the scents – blood from Rajit, blood from her head, blood from Etienne. The smell of the insanity of the Legends, of violence now and violence from before, of someone's horror so powerful that she began to shake. Her eyes were open, but she wasn't seeing and then strong hands lifted her up and a golden scent filled her, wiping away the scent of blood and violence.

"Marielle, stay with me. Marielle!" She felt her veil being torn from around her face and bound around her head and she was laid against something – a rock perhaps. The ground was cold beneath her but the hands tending her were gentle.

"You shouldn't be here, you know," Tamerlan's voice was low and soft under the noises of the fight. "You never should have been here among madmen and death. You should have lived and died an officer of Jingen. Maybe married a nice Watch officer and had sweet purple-eyed children. Stay here, love." She felt his lips press to her head. "I must finish this first then we'll look at that wound again."

She could smell spices burning, drifting in the wind. His smoke. His spice. He was nearly out of it, but here he was, using it again. He coughed and his smell morphed away from that pleasant, addictive gold to harsh elderberry as if someone had taken the astringent smell and fermented it badly. Legend.

But which Legend had him this time?

"Want to dance, pretty girl?" he called to Liandari.

It must be Lila Cherrylocks.

Her last emotion was jealousy as she slipped into unconsciousness.

19: INTO THE DARKNESS

TAMERLAN

Tamerlan stubbed out the roll of spice so he could use the rest later, tucking it into the pocket in his sleeve. He leapt forward – or rather Lila did. He'd been careful to take in only the barest whiff of smoke – just enough to call her – but not for long.

I don't need long!

Etienne jabbed at Liandari, his blade snaking in under her guard and slicing her inner thigh. Blood – bright red against the white snow – spurted out too quickly but Lila wasn't looking at that. What was she doing? She was supposed to come and help him!

Sure. When you call me for longer. For now, I'm going to help myself. Should have thought of that when you chose to only take one puff of smoke. Next time, call me for longer and we'll do what you want, too. It's always better when both parties are satisfied, don't you think?

He shivered internally at her suggestive mental tone, but it didn't affect his actual body. Lila stepped forward smartly, raised his sword and before he realized what she was about to do she was already bringing down the hilt toward Etienne's head.

"No!" Jhinn screamed from the boat and Etienne spun, the hilt missing his head.

His hand slammed up, gripping Tamerlan by the throat. Etienne shoved all his energy into the battle, shoving him backward as he slid against the snow.

Lila vanished from his mind with a curse and he let his limbs go limp, let Etienne throw him to the ground and waited there, panting, as the last tendrils of her faded.

Remember, next time, more smoke. Or it will go like this again.

He wasn't going to be blackmailed by her.

Of course, you are. You're nothing without us. Just a failed apprentice of a useless occupation.

"I hate it when you smoke that stuff," Etienne spat. He was quivering with emotion. "You're only feeding them. Only making it worse until one day you'll be as possessed as she is."

Etienne turned and prodded Liandari's body with the toe of his boot.

"She isn't dead, so maybe you could keep from kicking her, hmmm?" Tamerlan suggested, scrambling to his feet and hurrying to Liandari's side. He checked the wound in her thigh first. It was bleeding too much and too fast. He wasn't sure if he could bind it fast enough, wasn't sure if that would be enough. Had Etienne nicked the femoral artery? That would mean she'd die in minutes, right? Maybe if he was fast, he could save her.

He reached into her belt pouch with trembling hands, looking for needles, a bandage, whatever he could find. There was a scarf. Belatedly, he remembered he had a needle and thread of his own in his belt pouch. He dragged out the supplies slicing the leg of her breeches to access the wound.

Not good. Not good.

Thick red blood bubbled up so fast that he couldn't get a clear look at the torn flesh of her leg.

"What's wrong with Marielle, Tamerlan," Etienne said. His voice had calmed down. He was cold as the snow now.

"Her scalp was cut in the fight. It's not a deep wound, just bloody. I think she was light-headed from blood loss. Maybe lack of sleep, too. I set her to the side and bandaged her wound." He'd said it all while readying the needle for Liandari. He didn't know what he was doing. It made his hands shake.

"You're wasting your time here, Tamerlan. We want her dead anyway, or have you forgotten that a Legend lives within her?"

He looked up at Etienne – only a glance – only to judge his expression before returning to his work. He set the first stitch, feeling jittery with nerves as he pulled it tight. He didn't think it would be enough.

"I know you hate me because I smoke."

194

"You're addicted to the one thing that can destroy the world – the Legends." His voice twisted with bitterness. "Yes. It concerns me. It should concern you, too, or are you evil as well as a fool?"

"You know I'm not." The second stitch ripped. He bit back a curse. The flesh here was weak and he felt like stitching wasn't going to do enough. If a blood vessel was torn – shouldn't he be stitching that? But he didn't know how to. Sweat formed across his forehead. "You also hate me because Marielle doesn't."

"She deserves better than an insane lover. You will only ever drag her down."

"You were going to kill her," Tamerlan objected, trying again. This time the stitch held. He wiped his forehead with the back of his hand, tasting acid in his mouth. What else could he do but try? But there was too much blood soaking the snow around them and her breaths were too shallow.

"Anglarok," she murmured, her voice weak.

"Shhh, it's only me. Stay calm," he said setting the third stitch.

"And if I had succeeded it still would have been a better fate than loving you. Yes, I am beginning to hate you. Because you're a threat to me and to everyone and eventually someone will have to kill you."

"That's not enough reason to hate me. There must be something more." There. That stitch was holding. Not that it was helping. His hands were coated now in blood – as if he'd washed them in it. "Hold on, Liandari."

"Stop fighting the inevitable. It's a waste of your time," Etienne said as in the background Tamerlan heard Jhinn saying the same things Tamerlan was saying, only to his brother – soothing words of hope in the tight voice of someone trying to fight for a life.

"That's the difference between me and you, Etienne," Tamerlan said. "You see the world through calculating logic. And that's a very useful thing. But it means you give up when you shouldn't. And that makes you less human. Because I refuse to say that anything is inevitable. You can always fight. You can always hope."

"You're a fool. Just like your father. There's no hope for you, Tamerlan. Your addiction is going to kill you or kill us all. It's only a matter of time. What do you think will happen when we've chained all the dragons again – what do you think we'll have to do to the last vessel of the Legends? One way or another, this story ends in your death."

Tamerlan bit his lip and then glanced up at Etienne again. "You hate me because you know that's true for you, too. The Grandfather still has a link to you. If I have to die, maybe you do, too."

"Not if I destroy him in his clock. Not if I replace him with something else. But there's no fixing this for you, Tamerlan. You're infected by too many Legends. You will have to die. And if I have to be the one to kill you, I will. So, stop making Marielle fall in love with you. It's only going to hurt her more when we have to put you down like the rabid dog that you are."

He said it so coolly – like he was remarking on the weather.

"And until then?" Tamerlan asked, trying to keep his voice light.

"Until then, I will use you to do what must be done to save our people."

"That works for me," Tamerlan bit off the end of his words but Etienne was already striding away.

"Will your brother live, Waverunner?" he called to Jhinn.

Tamerlan's hands shook as he tied the last knot. The bleeding had slowed almost to a stop. He felt a slight flutter of a smile around his lips. Yes. Good. He'd made the bleeding stop. See? Nothing was inevitable.

His gaze drifted up to Liandari's face and he froze.

Son of a Legend! Her eyes were glazed over. The steam coming from his mouth and nose with every breath was missing. He reached up and put his hand just above her nose and mouth.

No breath.

The bleeding had slowed because her heart wasn't pumping blood anymore.

He sat back, letting his hands fall to his sides. He didn't care that he sat in snow redder than summer roses. Didn't care that her heat was steaming up in the pool of blood around her and fading into the air. Etienne had been right.

Despair and bitterness shot through his heart as his gaze drifted across the sleeping dragon mountains and the cold lake. Was Etienne right about everything else, too?

His gaze drifted to Marielle.

No. Nothing was inevitable. There was always hope. He stood up, rinsing his hands in the freezing cold of the lake until it felt like pins were being shoved under his skin as the cold of the lake sapped the life out of them.

With a sigh, he looked to the gondola where Etienne and Jhinn were arguing over what to do with Rajit.

"If you don't get him warm, he won't survive that. He should be on the land," Etienne was saying.

"There's something that way in a cave," Tamerlan said, interrupting them. "Given the warnings posted, it's likely what we came for."

Etienne grunted.

"And I think the lake extends under the rock into the cave."

Jhinn smiled at him, understanding what he meant.

"I think," Tamerlan said, giving Etienne a pointed look. "That we should put Marielle in the gondola, too, and then go into the cave and Jhinn can join us by way of water once we've scouted the path. It will be easier to transport the wounded on a boat."

Etienne gave him a cold look, but after a moment he shrugged. Tamerlan lifted Marielle as gently as he could, wading into the lake to bring her into the boat. He fussed with her cloak for a moment, pillowing her head and arranging the cloak warmly around her. Jhinn was loading the brazier with wood as

Etienne brought it to him. They placed the brazier close to Marielle and Rajit.

"How bad is his chest wound?" Tamerlan asked.

Rajit merely groaned.

"It's not deep, though I think she hit bone. It was a slash, though, not a stab and I stitched it. He's uncomfortable, but he should survive as long as there is no infection."

Tamerlan nodded. "Can you watch them both and go under the lip of the rock over there while we go on foot into the cave?"

Jhinn looked nervous. "I don't like it. The ceiling of rock will be very low – I'll barely be able to see over the gunwales. Why don't you check the cave first and then come back and tell me it's safe enough to bring the injured through."

"That makes sense," Tamerlan agreed. "Do you have a lantern you can spare?"

Jhinn grabbed one of his gondola lanterns and handed it to Tamerlan. "Here. I only have one other left, so don't break it."

They shared a commiserating look and then Tamerlan stroked Marielle's hair gently. She looked younger when she slept. So innocent. He didn't like the idea of leaving her – even for a short time. He kissed her hair gently.

"I'm leaving now," Etienne called. "if you expect to come, too, you'd better move it."

Tamerlan rolled his eyes, sharing another weary look with Jhinn and then he lit the lantern and followed Etienne toward the caves, nervously touching his pocket where he still had three and a half rolls of spice left.

Save them, Tamerlan, he told himself. Save them for when you really need them.

20: WHAT THE LADY SACRIFICE DIED TO HOLD

TAMERLAN

You must stop this foolishness, pretty boy! Lila's voice had been getting louder. And she wasn't the only one. Deathless Pirate broke in.

So far, we have kept you intact, helped you in your aims, worked for you when called. But that will end if you enter these caves. Do you know what it will be like to have an enemy inside your own mind?

Ram was resigned. *Perhaps it is not the worst thing to show you — to let you see what you must do. And why you must do it. You will see, as I did, that this is the only way.*

Etienne was reading the runes on the walls, taking his time as he examined each one.

"Do you want me to interpret these for you, Alchemist?" he asked coldly as he read.

"I can read them just fine on my own," Tamerlan said. Etienne's surprised expression was enough to give him a small, cynical smile. "You didn't think I could read?"

"Not the runes of the Dragonblooded."

"You know I am the son of a Landhold. I had his libraries at my disposal."

The former Lord Mythos sounded bored. "I know all the Landholds surrounding Jingen and have met the sons of most of their families. I can name only two others who can read the runes of the Dragonblooded. If you truly can read them, then you must realize that these runes were not made for the people of the river plains. They were laid out for the dragonblooded."

Because only the dragonblooded would open up the mountain with their blood, so they're the only ones who would need to read the warnings, Ram suggested. He would know. He was the one who had been there before.

You should prepare yourself.

For what? He put his hand on the hilt of his sword. They were at the place where he had heard the scream last time and turned around. The bend in the path was just ahead. Strange bumps covered it and steam rose up, sulfur perhaps, steaming up from holes in the earth as he'd read in his alchemist books. The path sloped down from the bumps in a strange shape that wasn't exactly flat. A ridge ran down the middle of it. The ridge was too bumpy to walk on, so they each took a side of the path. It was steamy here, warmer than in the outside air.

You have never been happy to see the Legends' avatars in the past. You may not like this one, either.

Avatar?

What did you think Anamay was? Just an innocent victim?

They turned the bend and Tamerlan gasped. This was more than a cave. The ceiling here opened up and he realized it was a place between dragons. A narrow pass for lack of a better word. There was no sign of water. This wasn't where the passage from Jhinn's lake went. The path led between the matched haunches of two dragons up ahead. But here, in this small gap carved out between the mountains, bright light shone above them and snow coated the ground of the sheltered mountain pass. Tall, smooth scaled walls – or rather dragon haunches, lined the pass. The only ways in or out were the two entrances – one from this cave – or whatever it really was – and one leading out the other side. The mouth of their cave sloped downward, still ridged but dropping off suddenly. The only problem was that the way between the two sides fell away into emptiness.

Well, not the only problem. He'd been trying not to look at the other problem.

Hanging from the ceiling at the end of the cave, the cold white light streaming around it – was a chained figure hanging upside down so that ghostly hair streamed in the winter wind.

Tamerlan shivered in horror. Loose chains jingled musically as they banged against each other and the smell of death was heavy in the cave.

Etienne shook his head, confused, he covered his face with the collar of his coat. "This body smells fresh."

There was a tinkling sound of something hitting the ground and Tamerlan swallowed down bile. Bright green emeralds leaked from the throat of the dead woman, forming a pile under her stinking corpse. Why did it stink when her blood was emeralds?

Avatars are part human, part magic, and part fantasy. What did you think would fall from her ravaged neck? Blood?

"She really wore the dress," he said, feeling stupid as he said it. But she was dressed in a silky white sheath as if she'd come here for a dinner party rather than a hunting party. Her eyes were empty holes filled with green stones and her open mouth was packed just as tightly with emeralds. He shuddered. "I thought it was just a picture – like the ones of her draped over a dragon snout."

"Where did you think the steam was coming from?" Etienne asked dryly.

He was right. They had walked down the snout of a dragon and they were standing on his head. The Lady Sacrifice had literally been slaughtered over his snout like in the picture he'd seen all that time ago in the Queen Mer library.

But why the dress? That still seemed strange. Why the emeralds?

What do you care? Ram the Hunter asked.

"Why so fresh?" Etienne asked, curiously. "Centuries later and we still smell the putrefaction?"

"I think that when she took Anglarok as her avatar she left this avatar," Tamerlan said. "When he died, she died. But this avatar was abandoned days ago. It's been actually dead for that long, not for the centuries it remained here."

Etienne cursed softly. "Was that in the book?"

"Sort of."

He cleared his throat as if trying to clear away the grisly scene. He pointed toward the open entrance over the cavern beyond.

"How did Ram get over that gap?"

"He killed a girl named Anamay and hung her up where you see her rotting corpse right now."

"Son of a Legend. That's grim."

"And you think I'm insane," Tamerlan commented quietly.

"We're not doing that," Etienne said quietly.

"Of course not," Tamerlan agreed. "But we also can't leap that gap."

"How did killing her bridge the gap?" Etienne asked, confused. "That part doesn't make sense to me."

It didn't make sense to Tamerlan either.

Magic is fueled by blood. Give it blood and it responds. But only the blood of the Dragonblooded. The people of the plains never had any magic in them. And I didn't kill her to get over the gap. I told you the book was wrong.

Well, he wasn't going to kill Marielle. Or himself. And no one else here was dragonblooded.

She was killed to hold the guardian of this place captive. Just as all the Legends do. We only used a drop of her blood to cross the bridge – that's where the book got it wrong. We killed her on the way back. To bind the dragon.

The ground rumbled beneath them.

I guess her replacement avatar – Anglarok – was still holding him in place. I didn't know for sure that could happen. But you killed him hours ago now.

Tamerlan shivered.

And that means the dragon is preparing to rise again. Unless you plan to kill someone to bind it?

Tamerlan felt like he was going to be sick. Every single action. Every act of mercy. Every act of hope. They all had a price.

You should cross the bridge while you can – if you dare.

"Are the voices in your head telling you differently?" Etienne asked. His voice was taut. And no wonder. He must hate having to ask when he hated what Tamerlan was doing with the Legends so much.

"Her death didn't open the Bridge," Tamerlan said. "It held down a dragon. It stirs now that Anglarok has been killed."

206

"By you."

"Yes."

Etienne's look was dark.

Tamerlan sighed. "Let's just cross the bridge, shall we?"

The book said that Ram had gone into the shadows and come out with an answer. Tamerlan scanned the opening of the cave and the walls. Was there –?

There. A shadowed alcove mostly hidden by rock. He raised the lantern and entered it cautiously. There was a metal plate set into the rock and nothing else.

Shaking his head, he slit his finger with his knife and let the blood drip onto the plate.

"You can come out now," Etienne said from outside the alcove. He was trying hard to disguise the awe in his voice. "Your blood has done its job."

Tamerlan stepped out of the alcove and his own jaw dropped.

A Bridge of air spanned the gap. You could only tell it was there by the subtle way it bent the light so that the landscape seen through it didn't quite look right. Along the edges, a faint light glowed, as if to warn those crossing not to step right off of it.

Etienne leaned down, gathered a handful of blowing snow and threw it at the bridge. The light dusting of ice particles coated its ephemeral form wherever the snow landed. Taking a deep breath, he planted a single foot on the bridge, testing his weight.

Tamerlan pushed past him, stepping onto the bridge without testing it.

"If you don't believe in magic by now," he said as he passed the other man, "then you haven't been paying attention."

21: Journey of Faith

MARIELLE

The sound of lapping water against the side of a boat woke her and she sat up. Stars flashed across her vision and her head spun so quickly that she fell back again.

"Easy," the word was gentle but concerned. "Easy now. It's not a bad wound, but it bled a lot. Maybe you should drink some tea. It's fortifying. The kind my grandmother used to give me."

"Jhinn?"

"Yes. It's me, girl. Jhinn. We're in my gondola."

She tried to sit again. This time taking it slowly.

"Careful. Don't want to knock over the brazier or the gondola will catch on fire."

She smelled the fire now that he mentioned it – smoky and woody, smelling of burning cedar. The lake – a mineral smell mostly, hardly even organic. If she had to guess, she'd say they wouldn't catch fish here. This lake barely even smelled alive.

And Jhinn – smelling of strawberry genius and hot, sudden flashes of smoked paprika – worry.

"What are you worried about?" she asked, groggy. It took her a moment to remember that she'd been hit with Liandari's sword. She hadn't dodged quickly enough. She looked around her. Rajit lay beside her, his fur cloak wrapped around him. From the pallor of his face and the sweat on his brow, she guessed he'd been wounded, too.

"If the boat burns down, I die," Jhinn said simply as if speaking to a child. "That's why I'm worried about you knocking over the brazier."

"No," Marielle said, shaking her head. "I don't mean that. I can smell you're worried. What's wrong?"

She was looking further now. The beach they'd fought on was a long way off. She could just make out the broken cart – and a heap of cloth on the ground nearby. Liandari. Or at least, her body. It was Abelmeyer who had controlled her. The one-eyed King. He'd been so powerful when she was in the clock. It was shocking to think of him as gone.

Jhinn had their gondola pulled up against the side of what could only be a large rock, though the water seemed to flow under it and from where they sat, almost tucked under the rock, it looked like you could float a long way under the rock – maybe a really long way. The light ended before the way clear did, and she smelled something – fresh air. Moving air. It wasn't stagnant under here. The air and water could move.

"Are you planning to go under this rock?"

Her question only made him more agitated. He fiddled with his little motor on the back of the boat. The pedal one. Had it broken in all the madness? She didn't think so. It looked whole from here.

"Tamerlan was supposed to come back and tell me if it was safe to go under this part of the dragon," he said and as he gestured above, she realized she could see a scale picked out on the rock in the light of the lantern. It was hard to make out. Just like the shore was. Which meant this was almost night. "That was many hours ago. And he has not returned. I'm reluctant to go. What if I do, and a moment later he comes flying around the corner to tell me it is not safe to take you and Rajit there? I worry not for myself, only for you and him. Tamerlan made me swear I would take care of you."

"And you have."

He nodded jerkily. His anxiety growing with her words, not reducing. It was all she could smell now.

"But it's been a long time. And this passage leads somewhere. What if he needs my help? What if by delaying, I am wasting the time I would need to help him?"

She nodded. Yes, she understood the dilemma.

"Perhaps you will go after him on foot? You can see if he is in trouble? If he has word about the passage here?"

She shook her head. "Your brother doesn't look well."

"He's not. I worry his wound is infected."

She nodded. "And you cannot leave the boat."

211

"No." He sounded a strange combination of certain and defeated.

"I think I should stay with you for now, Jhinn. And I think we should try this passage. What if I pedal and you stay at the bow and watch for trouble? We can turn around if the passage narrows or the current speeds up."

He nodded, reluctantly though. Clearly torn.

"We have to take a chance one way or another," Marielle said. "And I think I'd rather take a chance at being brave than at being foolish, don't you?"

"Yes." His eyes met hers, looking for support and she smiled encouragingly.

She still felt shaky as she took her place at the stern of the boat on the little seat Jhinn had made, pedaling to power the boat. He set himself up in the bow, pole in hand, ready to push aside any obstacle he could.

"Ready?" she asked.

"Yes."

She began to pedal, and in minutes the lake behind them was lost and all they could see was within the circle of golden light provided by the lantern and the open brazier.

Worry crawled through Marielle's own belly and she hoped they'd chosen correctly. If not, no one would ever find their bodies.

22: WHERE JOURNEYS TAKE US

TAMERLAN

They'd crossed the magic bridge hours ago and now Tamerlan was beginning to worry. The lantern was low on fuel. He tapped the base, swallowing at how little fish oil sloshed in the bottom of the lantern.

He should have turned back by now to tell Jhinn what was happening, but he just kept thinking that if he went a bit further he'd have something to report. And the further he went, the further he would have to go back just to tell his friend to stay put. Hopefully, Jhinn would know to do that on his own.

"They hacked their way through the rock here," Etienne said uneasily. Tamerlan raised the lantern higher, unsettled by where the gouges in the rock looked more like the work of metal claws than tools.

He took a step toward them, nearly tripping over a skeleton. When the book had said that Ram had only returned with half of those who went with them it hadn't said how the others had died. And Tamerlan still didn't know – but he was pretty sure

213

he knew *where* they died – here in this long, winding passage that led downward into the earth.

On the other side of the bridge, they had walked right underneath the frozen, gaping jaws of a dragon, their heads almost brushing his great throat as they crept down into the earth. It was not a path – not a mine or a man-made cave but just the gaps between dragons. The only sign that they were headed in the right direction were the dead. The treasures they had taken out of the earth lay with them. Golden coins he didn't' recognize. Jewelry more extravagant than any he'd ever seen. Gem-encrusted sword handles. Strings of pearls. Even shells like Marielle's yellow conch. There was a lot of evidence of fleeing people dying as they went – that and the signs of metal tools against dragon scales.

Tamerlan and Etienne hadn't touched the wealth. They didn't even speak of it. Likely, Etienne knew as well as he did that it would only weigh them down.

"I think the lantern is getting low on fuel," he said, swallowing down a burst of fear.

"Do you want to go back? Are you starting to see how foolish you are to think you – an alchemist's apprentice – can save the world?"

"I think the Grandfather is driving you mad," Tamerlan said mildly. "I knew an Etienne who was cool and calculating – yes – but he was also clever and self-sacrificing and determined. You are not him. You are unfocused and you aren't thinking things through. You know we both have to find a solution and that we are trying to do that right now."

Etienne spun, fire in his eyes, a hand raised as if to strike. Then he shook himself and nodded gravely.

"You may be right. And yet, he never stops, never relents, never ceases."

"I know."

Do you know? Deathless Pirate's voice in his mind was tinged with laughter. He and the others never stopped talking, suggesting, ordering or trying to seduce him into bringing them back. Never, not for even a moment, though he was getting better at ignoring it.

Etienne gave Tamerlan an accusing look, sharp and angry, but after a moment it faded, and he just shook his head.

"I feel magic up ahead. A lot of it. I think we should keep going. There isn't enough fuel in your light to get us back, anyway. Our only hope is ahead."

His hand drifted up to touch the gouges in the scale above him.

"What do you think happened here?" Tamerlan asked, horror in his voice. "It looks like – a battle against the rock itself. The scales, themselves I suppose. Do you think they were trapped here and had to cut their way out?"

"Yes."

"What makes you think so?"

Etienne's eyes sparkled with a strong emotion that he was trying to suppress. "The Grandfather has seen this time. He tells me the dragon was not frozen when they took this journey. Not completely."

"That's why they killed her," Tamerlan said, understanding filling him at the thought. "The Lady Sacrifice – Anamay. They killed her to bind it, didn't they?"

"Yes."

Tamerlan nodded with him and they were both silent then as they negotiated a difficult climb down a steep, too-smooth wall of stone. The passage was tight here and it was all Tamerlan could do not to panic as the rocks felt like they were closing in.

Soon you will understand. Soon you will see.

Why couldn't Ram just tell him? Wouldn't that save a lot of trouble?

I wanted you to listen. I didn't want you to come here. But since you are here, you should see for yourself – see why we fight. See why you must replace the avatars and bind the free dragons. Why you must destroy them utterly.

His voice seemed louder in Tamerlan's head. And it made sense that they should bind the dragons. There were so many here – if they ever slipped loose of the magic holding them – well, he didn't want to think of what would happen.

DESTRUCTION! DEATH! CHAOS!

His thoughts spiraled away and he stumbled. He barely heard Etienne cursing, though he felt the other man pulling him to his feet.

They killed Salamay here. See where he lies? The dragon crushed him under his great weight. He fell as we fled. I wanted to go back but I dared not. I alone carried the great shell. I alone had the power to bind them.

Tamerlan could see a man being crushed under the bulk of a dragon's belly as his friends tried to hack him free – tried and failed. He gasped. Salamay. He remembered the man. He'd loved beef stew and girls with brown eyes.

But that wasn't his memory, was it? It was Ram's.

Tamerlan was staring at a skeleton. A skeleton with a crushed skull. Someone was yelling at him. But he could see Salamay's face on the skeleton. See it as it was crushed under the dragon. He shuddered.

Yes. They had to stop this madness before more innocents were killed. Ram was right. He'd always been right.

He had a vague feeling that the other Legends were screaming now, trying to plead a different case, but he wasn't listening because of course they were wrong and obviously Ram was right.

He would go and see for himself and learn how to make the avatars that they needed to make. It was the only way.

"Tamerlan! Tam! Legends take it! Listen to me!"

He surfaced from his thoughts to see Etienne's worried face swimming in the light. He blinked and the face became clear.

"Are you with me? Dragon's spit, Tam! Pull yourself together. You are Tamerlan Zi'fen, Alchemist's apprentice. You are not

Ram the Hunter, do you hear me? You will not be making avatars."

"Did I say that?"

"Yes," his tone was terse as he dragged Tamerlan along. He had the lantern now. His eyes were bright in its light, almost feral as he pulled Tamerlan along and his own flowing words were as worrying as the Legends' were. "Just a little farther. I can feel it. I can feel the power. A little further. It burns my nose. It tickles my blood. It's here, close. Here. Enough to escape. Enough to be free."

If they were both going mad, then how would they keep each other sane?

There was a faint light ahead. Ram's excitement filled him and he hurried forward.

Here. We're here! I see the light!

Was that his thought or Ram's? Did it matter anymore? Their purpose was one. Their dream the same. Etienne was running beside him, gasping for breath as fast and furious as Tamerlan. Maybe it just made sense to be this excited. His eyes held a wild look – half-intensity, half-madness.

They emerged into a cave so large it could hold the city of Jingen. And at the end of the cave furthest from them a crescent of light – like a crescent moon – dipped so low that its lower edge skimmed the city's skyline. Water flowed out of it as if the moon itself could cry a waterfall into the city.

They paused, both of them awed to stillness as they looked at the great moon, While only a bare crescent was open and gushing water, the barest hint of an outline showed the rest of the circle against the blackness of the cave. It was large enough for a dragon to easily fly through, large enough to hold an entire city.

Despite the distance, he could hear the flow of the water pouring down the waterfall. The acoustics in this cavern must be amazing. Perhaps the dragons arching over them had landed in just the right spots to make a sound carry through the entire opening.

His eyes were adjusting to the light slowly. And as they did, his sudden gasp was a twin to Etienne's.

A city lay before them. Dark and massive. It spread out across the floor of the cavern – easily visible from where they stood on a ledge above it. Street upon street linked to square upon square. Endless rows of dark buildings, flowing bridges, soaring palaces, and carved terraces filled the empty space stretching from where they stood to the crescent far beyond.

"The Dragonblooded," Etienne gasped, catching Tamerlan's eye. "Your ancestors. This must have been one of their cities."

Nothing stirred below.

But as his eyes continued to adjust they grew larger.

There was a pedestal on the ledge nearby. Tamerlan set the lantern down on it almost absentmindedly and stepped out of its sphere of light to get a better look.

He couldn't believe his eyes.

"Are those —?"

"People?" Etienne finished. "Thousands of them. Standing in rows along the streets. Men, women, children. They are still as statues."

"Are they —?"

But he couldn't say the rest. Not when his blood was frozen as ice.

"Dead?" Etienne asked. "I do not know."

Tamerlan turned back for his lantern and realized it was not alone on the pedestal. Beside it, a book – the largest book he'd ever seen – stood on the pedestal, locked by a heavy iron lock with gears surrounding it. It looked like something Jhinn would build.

Absently, he stroked the cover of the book, his wound from when he opened the bridge catching on one of the gears and opening again. He cursed quietly, sticking his finger into his mouth to soothe it but the blood had already spread across the page.

The lock clicked and fell away and of its own accord, the book opened and settled on a page that read in the runes of the ancients: READ ME.

He turned the page and began to read aloud, the acoustics of the cavern carrying his voice – he was almost sure – completely across the entire city.

23: A Voice in the Darkness

MARIELLE

"I wonder if we made a mistake coming here?" Marielle said finally. She'd been wanting to say it for hours now. As the low-ceiling passage had gone on it had branched several times but though they'd marked their path she wasn't sure that she could find her way back even with the marks. And the water was flowing more quickly now, taking them downstream with a speed that she wasn't sure they could counter if they tried to turn the gondola around. Her pedaling had slowed until eventually, it had stopped completely.

"Probably," Jhinn agreed. His face was pale in the flickering light of the lantern. The brazier fire had run out of fuel an hour ago, though fortunately, the air here was warm – almost too warm for the fur cloaks. They wouldn't freeze to death – though at this rate they might plunge over an underground waterfall.

Marielle swallowed. "I don't think we can turn around."

"Not successfully. Any move now will only capsize us. I think we should change seats. Let me steer the boat and take the motor out of the current. You can watch for obstacles. Hmmm?"

His voice was like the skin stretched over a drum.

"Yes," Marielle agreed, waiting for him to come back and take the tiller before she moved forward, pausing to check on Rajit. He moaned lightly, sweat forming on his brow. Fever. He was not well. If he survived another day – well, he probably wouldn't. She glanced nervously back at Jhinn wondering if he knew.

She shouldn't have glanced back. His eyes grew big and he barely managed to shout "Duck!" to warn her.

She obeyed immediately, flattening herself on the gondola deck floor. She twisted to look up and had to clench her teeth against a scream. The ceiling had come down suddenly to where it was scraping along the gunwales now and the sense of speed had increased.

There was no turning back. No way to even get an oar or rudder out of the boat to turn them one way or another. All they could do was hold on for the ride and hope they survived.

"Try to secure the gear!" Jhinn barked.

She felt confused, but direction as better than nothing. Trying not to choke on the scent of their combined fear, she scrambled to gather his things and jam them into the forward hatch. The brazier didn't fit. It would have to fare as well as it could. Jhinn had the motor tied against the stern with a rope and he crawled forward giving Marielle the end of another rope.

"Help me tie Rajit in place."

"I don't understand," she said, but she was obeying anyway, tying a knot to a securing ring as Jhinn wrapped the rope around his brother and secured it to another ring.

"Hold on to the rope," Jhinn gasped.

There was a squealing sound and then the lantern snapped off the forward ferro and with the crunch of wood being splintered, their light was snuffed out.

The bottom fell out from under their gondola and Marielle screamed.

Her scream seemed to go on forever and then the boat struck the water below and she thought they were going to capsize as they rolled completely underwater, and then all the way back into the air again.

She choked on water and then gasped fresh air. They were still moving - quickly. She could feel the air as it dried her face. She was soaking wet, the boat was filled with water at least four inches deep from what she was feeling, and they were still in the dark.

"Marielle?" Jhinn called.

She was trying to scent for anything she could find but a sudden blast of magic scent hit her, driving all scents of minerals or water from her mind. Magic – rich and pure and powerful smelling of lilac filling her vision with turquoise and gold sparks – was everywhere. The scent, as addictive as ever, blinded her to everything else as she drew it in, in, in.

"Marielle!" he sounded panicked.

"Here. I'm here," she gasped, barely able to get the words out before another blast of the potent scent hit her again. She didn't have a scarf to wind around her face and she didn't think she could take anymore. It was too much. Too much. And she wanted more.

"Try to bail with your hands if you can, Marielle. I think the ceiling is higher. I can't feel it."

"Yes," she agreed breathlessly. A task. She needed to do this task.

She began to bail – feeling useless as her hands barely held enough water with every scoop to do anything at all but better this than simply sinking into senselessness at the overwhelming scent of that magic.

"I wonder where we are."

"I wonder when we'll *stop*," Jhinn said more dryly.

Rajit moaned and Marielle remembered that he was unconscious.

"Can he breathe?"

"I have him propped above the water. But I can't tell if there is a hole in the boat. We need to bail, or he will certainly drown and us with him."

She agreed, working faster to try to help, though it didn't seem to lower the water level at all.

Long minutes passed and then Jhinn asked, "Do you see a faint light?"

"Yes." But it wasn't bright enough to be more than a trick of her imagination and she couldn't smell anything but magic here. Nothing at all. It was like being doubly blind. She could barely smell Jhinn's desperation and he was right beside her.

And then words flooded the cavern, echoing slightly but still there.

"It says, 'Read this.'"

"Tamerlan?" she gasped.

But there was no response. He couldn't hear her.

"I think he's out there somewhere but the sound must be echoing through the cavern," Jhinn said. They were slowing down. There was less of a tug on her hands when she accidentally hit the water as she bailed.

"These are the Chronicles of the Dragonblooded in their city of Vale Hylinthia in the mountains of Meridew. I am the last of the living in Vale Hylinthia. I grow weak. And so, it befalls me to tell the tale of the Dragonblooded and how we lost our lives and cities to the dragons of the stars. I tell this tale for those who may come after. I tell this tale to warn you. May you choose wisely when the dragons wake again. May you choose life and not death, freedom and not captivity, sacrifice and not selfishness."

"He's reading it," Marielle gasped.

"There's something different about the water, Marielle," Jhinn whispered hurriedly as Tamerlan paused for breath.

"What is it?"

"I'm struggling to explain."

"Is it still water?"

"Yes, yes of course but it's like the difference between saltwater and freshwater, only more so. More intense. Can you smell it?"

"All I smell is magic," Marielle replied. And it was true. She tried to pick out the water, but that was only magic, too. "Maybe don't drink it."

She tried to fill her hands, absently, but the water at the bottom of the boat was all but gone now. They weren't going to sink. Not yet.

"I'm just going to wet a cloth with it to soothe Rajit. He's burning up."

She didn't get a chance to reply because Tamerlan was speaking again, his voice filling the space.

"It was in the reign of King Ixtathres that we became most enchanted with magic," Tamerlan read. "Always a tool, it now became an obsession. We created great things. Beautiful things of art and power. Gardens of flowers sung to life. Music that made things flourish. Art that came alive and lived with us. Jewelry with great power – the power to take sight – or give it back. The power to bind a soul – or loose it. We reveled in our creativity. There was no end to what we could make, what we could enjoy, what we could love."

"Jhinn?" Marielle whispered as Tamerlan paused for breath. "Are you seeing what I'm seeing?"

In the distance, she thought she saw a glowing crescent moon.

24: WHEN FATE WE CALL

TAMERLAN

"In the final year of the reign of King Ixtathres – the city of Vale Hylinthia touched the stars," Tamerlan read. The lantern lit his pages, but he couldn't help but feel cold as he read.

Etienne climbed down the smooth lip of the dragon's tail on which the platform was built. He was walking now on the edge of the city, inspecting the people who stood in rows.

"They're like statues!" he called when Tamerlan paused for breath. "Perfect, cleverly detailed statues! Their skin is stone. Their clothing like stalagmites."

Tamerlan kept reading. "And so, we sought a way to the stars ourselves, a way to touch the power of the heavens, to travel the waters between the planes. And we found life there. For life is water and water is life, and the life we found was magic so much greater than ours that ours was only an echo of it.

"Our mages worked day and night, funded by the King, racing to find a way to carve out a path from the space between the worlds, the waters between the universes, and to navigate it.

We would be Legends. Gods among men. We would bridge the gap between man and the heavens – no – we would sail it. We would be free to go where we wanted, floating on the water of life."

This sounded like something Jhinn would love – like something, perhaps, that his people would relate to.

"There are tens of thousands of them!" Etienne called up. "I swear, I can almost feel them breathing."

Tamerlan shivered and turned the page.

"And so, we found the rhythm of the universe and we echoed it with the shell instruments we had carved for ourselves. We filled them up to use for the generations to come. And the final, greatest one, we turned back on the waters of life and we carved a great portal for ourselves and rejoiced as the waters of life flooded the canals of our city and danced down the mountains like wine from an overflowing goblet."

Tamerlan looked up at the crescent moon, pouring water and shuddered again. That was it, wasn't it? The portal they had carved. The way between worlds.

"But we had not considered the dragons."

He turned another page.

"I could spend all day here looking at these people," Etienne marveled. "Their clothing! Their gems! Tamerlan, it's right out of history!"

What do you think my men filled their pockets with when we fled this place? Were they not full of necklaces, bracers, and crowns? Did they not trip and fall over their own riches? It took money to fund my hunt. It took money to bring down the last of their kind.

Tamerlan swallowed down a burst of fear. He was standing in the largest tomb the world knew. The tomb of an entire city. Children had played here, and people had grown and lived and toiled and loved and then turned to stone forever here. Deep respect was owed to them, and deep fear. For whatever could turn this great city to stone and dust could turn all the world to the same.

He cleared his throat and read more.

"They came in a flood – the smallest of them the size of our city – poured into our mountain range like fish from a barrel shipped up from the south. We did not know how to stop them or what to do. Our magic was the magic of blood. And blood was the only way. We gave ours to imprison them. First, just one person made a Legend forever – suspended in the time that is not time between the dimensions. But one was not enough. Her hold was only temporary. And then her death was nothing because the dragon rose again."

Below him, Etienne had grown silent, though Tamerlan saw him still walking down the long portal-lit street.

"The dragons tried to turn us, invading our minds, twisting our thoughts. They turned those they touched mad with fear of the land and these clung to the water claiming it was life itself and none could move them from it. For they said that when the dragons left back through the portal, they would go with them. And we pled with them to take the dragons and go. To stop torching our farms and villages, stop feasting on our fleeing

231

people. But as many of our people fled to the plains, the people of the water told us that they could not go. For the dragons could not open the portal wide enough again without our help and could not close the portal again unless all their kind left together. And already one of them had snuck away and could not be found."

"In fear, we acted in haste. I, Dystanler Quarenspear was Lord Mythos of the City and keeper of the Mage Houses at that time. And so, I gathered together every mage from great to small and together we spoke to the King and in great turmoil, he made his choice. We sent all those out of the city who could be made to go. But those of us who ruled. Those who had the great blood running pure in our veins – those who had called to fate and tempted chance and opened the portal and brought the dragons – it was we, and our children, who chose to atone for our sin.

"And in that night, we made the entire population of our city a blood sacrifice and we banished the souls of our people to the neverlands where there is no Bridge back to this world. It was the price we paid to trap the dragons forever. Because if any of our people were to find the bridge and cross again the spell would be broken, and the dragons loosed, and all of this would be for naught.

"One by one, my mages fell until it was only I, Dystanler Quarenspear, left blowing into the shell and echoing the magic that felled the dragons and sealed them around our great city. Their bodies formed greater mountains and deeper caverns. Their hardened scales blocked the sun from what had once been the city of the stars.

"And I was the only one left to see what we had wrought in our haste."

Etienne was returning now, moving quickly through the street, a lantern in his hand. The lantern flickered with turquoise fire – as if lit by magic. Did Etienne have his magic back?

Tamerlan turned back to the page. He could see why Ram knew from this that he must quell the dragons. And he could see a bit of how he knew what to do, but was there more? Because there weren't any specifics on the exact way to make a person into a living avatar.

"When I realized what we had done, I walked through the city. Not everyone had been used to bind the dragons. Only those on the land. Those on the water remained, but they would not speak to me, claiming I was a dead man and no longer living. They fled the city by means of the river but I carved my own way out to the mountains high above and I formed a bridge to cross a chasm and tuned it to the blood of my people. And while I made the bridge a horrible sight came to my eyes – a dragon, still flying, still alive. We had missed some. I know not how many.

"And so, I returned to my city and I have penned this tome. To any who follows, I leave the tools we used to bind the dragons and this ledger to guide them. I will go from here and search for any I may stop, but my strength is weak and my magic fades when I cross the bridge into the mountains. I may not survive the journey.

"I plead with you, if you are reading this. Stop the dragons. Bind them to the earth. Do not let them destroy the world.

They killed us by the hundreds. They drank our magic until only the echoes were left. They destroyed our nation, our people, our children, our future.

"And they will do it to you.

"No amount of blood is too much to stop them. No sacrifice too great. You must be strong enough to stand against them. Mad enough to hope. Hard enough to take innocent lives to do what you must.

"Do not fail. Do not betray your blood."

25: AND FATE REPLIES

MARIELLE

"It's the story," Jhinn said, his breath held, his eyes so wide they were tearing up.

"What story?" Marielle asked puzzled by his joy – so strong and powerful that it even cut through the overwhelming scent of magic as it ripped through him. The scent of cherries and bright wafting cerise bursts spurted from him as he grabbed her hands.

"*The* story, Marielle. The story my people have been searching for since Queen Mer's day. The story that was supposed to make sense of everything!" His excitement was impossible to contain. He leapt to his feet and began to free the motor to power his boat. "It was all true. All of it. The dead on the land. The water being life – but not the water I was raised on. This water!" he scooped up a handful, flicking it across the boat. Rajit moaned as it splashed across his face. "It's life, Marielle. It always was. And we weren't meant to be on land, we were meant to sail between the worlds, to sail between the stars."

Marielle froze. This was crazy. Worse than Tamerlan or Etienne. She opened her mouth to say so and then shut it with a click.

She had no longing to sail in the blackness between stars. She'd choose earth over that any day of the week. She'd choose a dirty city and calling voices. If she was home right now – if her home still existed – it would be Winterfast. No one would be eating for a week, though everyone would drink fragrant teas. And they would think deeply about their history and their futures and give to the poor. And make vows. And they would remember the history of their people and how there was nothing to eat during the dragon famine when the descending dragons burned the farmlands. And they would honor the strength of their ancestors.

So, was it crazy that Jhinn wanted to honor his? Was it crazy that he wanted his own remembrance of history and hope for the future?

It wasn't crazy at all, was it? It all finally made sense of what he'd believed on faith his entire life.

"Are you going to sail through that crescent, then?" she asked.

"I can't. Didn't you hear what he said? The dragons are bound here, and they are the only ones who know how to ride those currents."

Which meant he wanted the dragons to wake.

A voice broke into her mind – too loud and harsh for her. She flinched in pain, rocking to her knees.

MARIELLE. JHINN.

No, it wasn't a voice. It was – a thought? A feeling?

HELP US.

Help who?

The gondola turned a corner and now the light of the crescent above them filled the city as they floated into it. The corner had turned them into one of the city's canals and as they floated up the canal Marielle saw the people – frozen stone statues of people in rows lining the canal. Their faces frozen in expressions of life – fear, sadness, joy, surprise – everything a real human face would look like. Only these people did not live. They only existed. Just like Jhinn thought her people did. She shuddered at the thought. Was it them calling to her?

The current was pulling them toward the Crescent moon – which didn't make any sense at all since water was pouring *out* of the crescent. It should be pushing them away from it. But with all the magic lingering in the air, anything was possible right now. Anything at all.

THE BOOK DOES NOT TELL THE WHOLE STORY.

She flinched from the voice in her mind.

It felt like a thousand little knives slicing through her brain. Like a thousand thorns scraping her skin from her bones.

She glanced at Jhinn through eyes watering with pain, but his eyes were gazing behind her at the crescent, a look of rapt attention on his face. Was he hearing the same thing?

OUR PERSPECTIVE IS DIFFERENT.

"Whose perspective?"

"Can't you see them?" Jhinn asked, wonder in his voice.

"See who?" She scanned the darkness, but all that she could see were the lines of staring stone people, dead and yet alive. They were so close here along the canal that she could pick out their cold, proud expressions. Every detail down to the eyelash was perfect as if these people only had to take a breath and they would be alive again.

"The spirits of the dragons," Jhinn said. "They're so beautiful!"

WE SWIM BETWEEN THE STARS – BETWEEN THE WORLDS – WITHIN THE WATER OF LIFE. WE CREATE BEAUTY AND PLACES FOR OTHER CREATURES TO LIVE WITH THE DARK ENERGY THAT HOLDS TIME TOGETHER. WE DID NOT COME TO HARM THIS WORLD. THE TEAR THESE CREATURES MADE IN REALITY SUCKED US IN. WE COULD NOT FIGHT THE PULL. AND THEN WE WERE HERE – HUNGRY, AFRAID, AND EVENTUALLY TRAPPED.

But they'd eaten people and burned cities, so she'd have to take this information in context.

WE ONLY WANT TO BE FREE – TO RETURN TO OUR PLACE IN THE SPACES BETWEEN THE STARS. THIS STRANGE WORLD MADE US INSANE. WE KNEW NOT WHAT WE DID, ONLY THAT WE WERE DESPERATE TO GO.

"All of you?" Marielle asked aloud. "Will all of you go if you can?"

IT IS ALL WE'VE WANTED FOR CENTURIES AS WE LAY HERE – CAGED WITHIN OUR FROZEN BODIES. ROCK THAT IS NOT ROCK.

"Will you take us with you?" Jhinn asked, seeming to hold his breath as he waited for the answer.

IF YOU COME, THERE IS NO LAND ON WHICH TO BUILD OR PLANT. ONLY WATER FOREVER.

"Yes," Jhinn said, excitement in his voice like Marielle had never seen before.

YOU WOULD BE WELCOME LITTLE ONE. AND YOUR PEOPLE, TOO. BUT WE CANNOT CLOSE THE PORTAL UNLESS EVERY DRAGON IS FREED.

Did that mean they were blackmailing Jhinn and Marielle into freeing the ones down on the plains? That would mean more cities destroyed, more homes gone, more people killed. Marielle gritted her teeth. But what did the Real Law think about creatures being trapped on a plane that wasn't theirs and stuck for centuries at the whim of other creatures who killed their own to keep them trapped? That didn't seem right or just, either.

IT IS NOT BLACKMAIL. IF YOU CAN OPEN THE PORTAL AGAIN AND FREE US, THOSE OF US WHO ARE HERE WILL CROSS OVER. WE WILL HOLD THE PORTAL OPEN UNTIL THE OTHERS ARE FREE AND THEN CLOSE IT AGAIN. YOUR WORLD WAS NEVER

MEANT TO TOUCH OUR PLANE. BUT YOU MUST FREE THE OTHERS. ALL OF THEM. OR THE PORTAL WILL REMAIN OPEN. AND ALL THIS WILL COME TO PASS AGAIN.

Marielle swallowed. It wasn't blackmail. And yet, it sort of was. To get rid of them, she had to free them. With no guarantee that they would go.

WE WANT TO GO MORE THAN ANYTHING.

"Of course, we'll free you," Jhinn breathed. "Right, Marielle?"

Marielle chewed her lip. Leave them trapped and they'd have to make more avatars and build more cities and kill people every year to renew the blood magic. Wait. How were these dragons trapped without a city on top of them or blood every year?

THE MAGIC USED HERE IS POWERFUL – THE SACRIFICE OF AN ENTIRE CITY. IT WAS ENOUGH TO HOLD US ALL. PERHAPS, THE MAGE THAT TRAPPED THE DRAGONS ON YOUR PLAIN WAS NOT AS POWERFUL. PERHAPS HE SACRIFICED FEWER SOULS AND HAD TO RESORT TO MORE PRIMITIVE WAYS TO RENEW THE BONDS.

That made a lot of sense.

Which meant she would have to go back to the plains and go against her conscience and sacrifice innocent souls year after year to keep these dragons trapped.

Or.

She could trust the dragons, find a way to open their portal, and set them all free. And all this would be over and done with. There would be no more dragons on the Dragonblood Plains. No more sacrifices. No more Legends and madness and horrific death.

"It sounds too good to be true," she said aloud. "Which usually means it is not true."

IT WILL REQUIRE A SACRIFICE.

"It would be worth it, Marielle," Jhinn said. They were so close to the crescent now that his face was brightly lit with it. He smiled beatifically in the bright portal-light.

Their gondola surprised her when it bumped up against a stairway. She looked up to see that the stairs spiraled around a central pillar. Bridges from the streets led to the pillar and at the top of it, on a wide platform, was the largest shell Marielle had ever seen. It was shaped like a conch, but larger than a ship.

MAGIC IS A MATTER OF WILL COMBINED WITH POWER.

Marielle was no mage.

ALL THE POWER YOU WILL EVER NEED IS COMING THROUGH THE PORTAL.

Which was true. She could smell the truth of it.

WE WOULD ASK THIS BROTHER OF THE WATER — BUT HE CAN NOT AID US IN THIS. ONLY SOMEONE WHO CAN CLIMB UP ON LAND CAN HELP US NOW.

241

"Please, Marielle," Jhinn said. "Just think, you can save the Dragonblood Plains and the whole world from the dark magic that has bound these dragons to us. And you can free my people to seek our place on the eternal seas."

Behind him, Rajit coughed and sat up. He looked – healthy. Healed. His eyes were huge with shock. He'd been listening, hadn't he? How shocking would it be to turn your back on your family's weird cult only to find out they'd been sort of right all along?

But how was he well?

A memory of Jhinn splashing water across the boat leapt to her mind. Some had landed on Rajit. Some had landed on her. He'd also bathed his brother's head with the magic-water. She felt her own head. The wound across her scalp was completely healed. Stunned, she pulled the bandage off her head, staring at the dried blood on it.

WE HAVE ALL THE POWER NEEDED. BUT WE NEED YOU TO HAVE THE WILL. SET US FREE.

So, she just had to climb up the steps and blow into the shell? The gondola bumped again against the lowest step. It would be easy to step off the gondola and mount the steps. Too easy. Nothing in life was so easy.

Jhinn rushed to his brother, speaking to him in a low voice as Marielle swallowed, looking up at the shell. They'd proven they had the power, but did she have the will?

YOU MUST WILL THE PORTAL OPEN. WILL US AWAKE AGAIN.

242

And what would that do?

YOU WILL HAVE TO MAKE A CHOICE. US, OR THE STONE PEOPLE BELOW. ONLY ONE OR THE OTHER MAY LIVE ONCE THE HORN IS BLOWN.

What did that mean? Right now, those people were stone – their souls sealed up to keep the dragons free.

THINK OF IT THIS WAY. WHEN YOU CHOOSE TO FREE US, YOU WILL BE FREEING THEM, TOO. FINALLY, THEIR SOULS MAY GO ON FROM WHERE THEY ARE TRAPPED. ON TO THE LIFE BEYOND. OVER THE BRIDGE OF LEGENDS TO THE LIFE BETWEEN THE WORLDS.

Where the dragons lived?

YES.

That didn't seem like much of an afterlife.

ONLY BECAUSE YOU DON'T UNDERSTAND ANY OF THIS. WE SPEAK TO YOU AS TO A CHILD. IT IS THE ONLY WAY TO TELL OF WONDERS AND LIFE YOU CANNOT YET COMPREHEND.

She stepped out of the boat. Not because she'd decided yet – she hadn't. She'd almost died in that gondola more than once. She just wanted to feel dry land under her feet again.

She was moving up the steps before she realized it, drawn by the pulses of sweeping magic scent washing down from the conch shell in waves of turquoise and sparkling gold. She remembered the first time she'd met the Lord Mythos and smelled that residue on him. Remembered when she'd smelled it on Tamerlan when she met him, too – a residue of the Legends he had smoked into existence.

And now here she was, mounting the steps to this conch about to make the biggest decision of her life. Would she use that addictive magic? Would she make a choice that would affect tens of thousands of people?

Her palms were sweating, her head hot and dizzy. She couldn't pull her thoughts into order. They were as scattered as when she went into the clock, jumping from memory to memory of her time in the lives of others through the past. She was ill with the choice set before her.

She'd seen how much caging the dragons had cost the people of the Dragonblood Plains. She'd seen how they had suffered under having to give their children to the dragons. She'd seen how the Legends had offered themselves to save their people.

And it would all happen again.

Unless she stopped it.

Right now.

She was at the top of the platform and she could see over the city. Her shadow, long and inky black, spread out over countless shops and homes and markets. Over palaces and canals, bridges and city squares. With the portal behind her, she loomed like destiny itself.

And beneath her shadow were row upon row of people who would never live again if she freed the dragons – except for in this new way she couldn't understand.

But hadn't they made that decision when they chose to become sacrifices in the first place? So why did she feel such a pang of guilt and pain at the thought of damning them to the next life while undoing their work completely?

Down the streets that fanned out before her, she saw movement and strained her eyes to see. Was that Tamerlan and Etienne rushing down the street toward where she was? It was hard to tell. They were still so far away that they seemed like nothing more than moving specks of shadow.

Perhaps, it was only her imagination tempting her with the thought of giving this horrible choice to someone else. She was the woman who acted, not the woman who chose. She was the woman who carried out plans, not the one who made them.

She turned and saw an empty shelf built into the side of the platform. It was large enough to contain many items, though it was empty now. Chiseled into the shelf were words she could not read.

No matter, she was not here for whatever had rested on those shelves. She was here for the great shell that filled the platform. With care, she followed the line of it to the narrow end, running her hand along its smooth surface as she went.

If she blew it, she would undo the work of centuries, destroy a part of the world to save the rest.

Did she dare do that?

This should be the decision of someone else – Etienne perhaps. He had been trained for this. Or even Tamerlan who was at least the son of a Landhold understanding the politics and history of this. Or Jhinn who believed all this through to his core – but it couldn't be Jhinn.

It should not be her.

It should not be a lowly watch officer the daughter of a red-door woman from the Trade District.

But if she left this decision to Etienne or Tamerlan, she couldn't be sure it would be them who made it and not the Legends who controlled them.

Who better to make a decision about justice than a member of the Jingen City Watch?

She had heard the story of this from both sides. Both sides had claims of injustice, of wrongful deaths, of wrongful imprisonment. Both sides had a proposal to make for the future.

So, which of them was right? Which should she rule in favor of? Which side lined up with the Real Law right now?

There was another small set of steps that led up to where a person could place their lips on that huge conch shell and blow.

Marielle climbed the steps, her mind racing so fast that she nearly tripped as she climbed them, and in the light of the bright Crescent moon portal, she stepped up to the conch shell and made her choice.

26: NEVER FAST ENOUGH

TAMERLAN

Tamerlan turned the next page, but there was nothing on it – nothing but a dark smear that looked like blood.

When we found the book, a fight broke out among us. A disagreement about how to proceed. Ram explained. He was still the only Legend voice Tamerlan could hear clearly. The others screamed and shouted in the background – fighting over something he didn't understand.

A disagreement that drew blood?

Belgarian thought that the dragons should be freed. He was mad – he would have doomed us all! I bashed his head in. A messy business. Blood spattered on the book.

Tamerlan shuddered.

Someone moves at the other end of the city! Look!

He looked. He thought he saw a gondola moving through the canals. But that was impossible.

A great danger lies there. You must stop the people in that boat before they reach it!

It wasn't Jhinn, was it? He was going to wait for Tamerlan to come and get him before moving from the lake.

Trust no one! No one!

There was a roar from the shadows as Etienne launched himself at Tamerlan and it was all he could do to leap out of the way, narrowly dodging the other man's attack. His sword flashed in the portal light and Tamerlan drew his awkwardly.

Smoke! Call me and I will come!

He didn't dare. Ram was too close already. His thoughts and desires already taking over too strongly.

"What are you doing, Etienne? We're on the same side!" His sword came up just in time to parry Etienne's attack – a sudden viper-like backhand slash toward Tamerlan's throat. "You're insane!"

"I know now," Etienne said, his face twisting. He looked more like the Grandfather like that than he did like Etienne.

"You don't know anything! We're on the same side! We're here to defeat the dragons and save our people!"

"Maybe I don't want them defeated. Maybe I just want their power."

"There's power here," Tamerlan said, feinting and then leaping back to grab the lantern from the podium. "Coming from that portal!"

"I know," Etienne said with a wicked smile. He held up a hand and lightning crackled between his fingers.

Run! It's the Grandfather!

Tamerlan didn't hesitate, he ran.

With a sword in one hand and a lantern in the other, running through an unfamiliar city was crazy. But he fled, sliding down the steep slope of the dragon's tail on his hip to land roughly on his feet. Maybe he would smoke.

Faster! Faster! Ram was screaming in his mind – or maybe his thoughts were. It was hard to distinguish one from the other anymore.

The rows of people stared at him inhumanly, sending thrills of terror through him even as he sprinted between them, his breath coming in gasps his legs screaming as he threw every ounce of energy into running.

He turned to look behind his shoulder, nearly skidding into one of the still figures – a hooded lady with a beautiful face and lips parted slightly in the faintest of smiles. It looked like she might exhale at any moment.

He gasped, but his turn had shown him Etienne right behind him, his feet pounding on the cobbles.

Tamerlan turned back toward the portal, slipping and skidding on the slick stone street, nearly losing his lantern. Ram forced him forward again. The Legend's power was taking him over every time he had the slightest moment of weakness. He pushed at it, but fighting it grew more difficult by the minute as he lost track of what was Ram and what was him. What were Ram's desires and hopes and dreams and what were his?

Run! They thought together. *Faster!*

He ran faster.

Smoke!

He was fumbling for the rolls of spice before he realized what he was doing. He jerked his hand away. If he did that now, he'd lose control entirely. He didn't dare. He didn't dare.

He –

A horn blast filled the air – loud and incredibly resonant. It shook through him so that his legs wobbled and he lost the lantern as he tried to keep his feet. It fell away, skittering across the cobbles and smashing to pieces, the light vanishing.

Tamerlan stumbled a step, grabbing a hold of one of the frozen people as he tried to keep his feet. It was a street vendor by the look of him – dressed in furs and with more furs in his hands held up like he was planning to make a last sale before his soul was stolen – an older man with a lined face and hooked nose.

Tamerlan took a deep breath. The world was calming. It was going to be okay. He just needed to stay calm.

He patted the statue absently on the shoulder.

The street vendor's eyes opened.

Tamerlan screamed, leaping back, knocking into Etienne. His sword flew from his grip and for a few desperate minutes ,there was nothing but terror and a deep sinking feeling in the pit of his belly as he scrambled wildly across the cobbles to retrieve it.

By the time he had his sword and was back on his feet, he saw Etienne leaping up, too, with his own sword in his hands.

None of the frozen people had moved. But all along the street, their eyes were opening.

Fear gripped his heart, forcing it into a staccato rhythm as he lifted a hand.

"Peace, Etienne. Don't fight with me. Whatever this is, we need to stop it."

He had the creeping sensation that the statues behind him were creeping forward in the darkness, coming to get him.

"I don't play by your rules, Hunter," Etienne said in a voice that sounded nothing like him.

Gulping down fear, Tamerlan leapt forward sprinting again toward the bright moon-portal, as hard as ever before, as if he could run fast enough to leave these nightmares behind. As if he could outrun the eyes watching him from every direction.

Something inside him was screaming like a frightened child. It was all he could do to shove it aside and run on.

He'd been running for an hour – or maybe it only felt that long. A stitch formed in his side, sucking his breath away when the next horn blast made the air shiver. He heard Etienne cursing behind him. The other man hadn't flagged.

Maybe it had been more than an hour. He'd started to taste blood in his mouth a while ago, felt like his lungs might explode a little after that, but still he'd run, fear giving him the strength he needed to keep going.

This horn blast was not a good sign. The last one had opened their eyes. What would this one do? He swallowed as the sound of a wind swirled in the air as the tone of the horn faded away. No, not a wind. It was the sound of thousands and thousands of people drawing breath.

He could feel fear-tears starting in his eyes. He blinked them away. He had no time to let fear steal his senses. He was already losing his mind as Ram chanted endlessly in his head.

Faster, faster, faster.

He ran on.

He didn't know how much more time had passed. Too long, he knew. He was limping now, barely able to keep stumbling along, too exhausted and sore.

He stumbled out into the open and saw a boat tied to a jetty. It was old and it knocked against the canal wall in the strong current that seemed – impossibly – to be flowing *toward* the waterfall at the other end of the city.

He didn't stop to think. He just leapt from the canal wall into the boat, cutting the rope with the blade of his sword rather than fumbling with the knots. The boat was moving the moment the rope was hacked apart, flowing down the canal faster than he could run.

At least this way he wouldn't have to worry about Etienne putting a sword through his back.

Faster, faster, faster.

He wasn't even rowing, and the boat was streaking toward the portal.

A massive pillar rose up in front of the portal bearing a shell so big it could be a ship on top of the pillar. What was that for?

It's the same as the smaller shells – a way to echo magic and transform it. There was a shelf full of smaller shells on that platform. I took them all and I used them. I found a way to do it without sacrificing an entire city – a way to use blood magic and a lesser shell to make a sacrifice of just one person to quell a dragon. Anamay was the first. But then the others followed. Some came to me willingly like Ablemeyer and Chaos. Others, I forced to serve – like the Grandfather and the Great Thief.

Tamerlan shivered. If he did what Ram was demanding, he would be forcing people to "serve" which was just a nice way to say "die."

Some will volunteer. That Scenter who works for you will volunteer. Mark my words.

Anger hardened in Tamerlan's heart.

He shoved against Ram, battering and fighting until he thought he was fighting his own mind. No one would do that to Marielle. No one! He would die a thousand deaths before he let that happen!

But as hard as he fought, he was losing, losing his mind inch by inch by inch.

The great horn sounded again and this time, the crescent moon of a portal above them began to enlarge, glowing brightly as it opened, opened, opened.

Oh no.

The water under his rowboat sped up, and now it was racing down the canal toward the tower faster than he'd ever seen a boat go before. In the distance, he saw another boat tied up at the base of the pillar and a familiar figure crouched within it. Jhinn? He was at the tower? How had he gotten here?

And where was Marielle?

As the last strains of the horn faded away, the people – formerly statues – changed again.

They began to sing. It was a low, urgent song. A dirge, he thought. The sight of a thousand frozen people, unmoving, grey and frozen in time, but singing the same song together, sent shards of icy fear through his veins.

This was a disaster.

This was the end of the world.

But was it him thinking that, or was it Ram?

If they were waking, then any moment now the dragons would wake, too. Hundreds of them – an entire mountain range of them. And what would he do then?

Die. We will all die together. The world will burn! Burn! Burn!

Ram was ranting in his head as the light of the portal grew unbearably bright and it swelled to a full moon – a bright round circle. Strange currents swirled in the pouring water that streamed out of it like a dam bursting.

Tamerlan barely had time to gasp and then his boat slammed into Jhinn's gondola and he trembled at the look of sheer awe in Jhinn's face.

"Isn't it amazing!" the boy gasped. His voice was full of joy. "She's setting them free."

Oh, sweet Legends!

You called? That was Lila. *Free us Alchemist! Let us stop this!*

But would they?

Freeing these dragons won't free us. The only dragon I want free is the one holding my soul captive – and only if you replace my avatar. No harm. No trickery. Just a simple exchange. Doesn't that seem pretty decent and honest compared to this madness?

He shoved her thoughts aside and leapt past Jhinn to the stairs mounting the tower.

The horn blasted again, and he flinched from it. His heart sank as he realized who it must be up on that platform. Who it must be who was destroying everything. But no, he didn't dare believe it.

Whatever happened next would be horrific. He could see in his mind the people of the city finally free and walking as one to surround him, to rip him limb from limb.

He shivered, aghast and not able to stop himself from turning to see what the horn had done.

He froze.

The song died on the lips of the masses, a silence – heavier than before – descending over them. The person closest to him – a teenage girl at the base of the tower looked up at him and he bit back a scream.

She lunged forward and then mid-movement, she slumped as if she were a sail with the ropes slashed apart, falling to the ground in a heap. Behind her, another person fell, and another and another, like dominos across the city.

He gasped.

No!

Tamerlan spun and raced up the steps, taking them two at a time.

Please don't be right. Please don't be right! He hoped with all his heart that he was wrong about this, that he had misjudged, that he was somehow blinded to an enemy within their midst.

He turned the last step and saw her there, her lips parted and her eyes wide as if waiting for something.

"Sweet Marielle," he gasped, his chest heaving as it tried to make up for all the breaths he hadn't taken as he raced across a city to her side. "What have you done?"

There was a rumble from above them like the movement of rock on rock.

"What have you done?"

27: Betrayal

MARIELLE

She turned, shocked to see him there. She was almost finished. The dragons were almost free. And when they were, she would have to flee this place or risk being killed as they fled this world. The magic, though only an echo had already taken its toll.

Her vision had narrowed as the edges darkened and closed in. Her sense of scent had been so overwhelmed with the fullness of magic that she hadn't smelled Tamerlan at all, didn't smell anything even now. And the pain – the pain tore through her as if it meant to break her bones inside her body and grind her to dust.

"What have you done?" he asked, his face etched with betrayal.

"I had to make a choice," she said, swallowing. Surely, he must understand. He'd had to make choices, too. He'd made choices that had destroyed cities. If anyone knew what that was like, wasn't it him?

But then why did he look like she'd taken his other eye?

He fell to his knees. Grief and then anger whipsawing across his face.

"You've killed them all, Marielle. All those people. Children. Parents. People who gave themselves to stop these dragons from hurting anyone else – and you threw that all away and destroyed them. How could you?"

A loud hiss like a waking snake filled the air and then a beam of light – bright as noon but narrow and shifting opened to them. The world seemed to flicker from shadow to light as she tried to focus on Tamerlan's face. The dragons were waking above the city. And they're movements were opening up the cave to the sky.

"I had to," she said, pleading for him to understand. "I didn't have a choice!"

"Of course, you had a choice! You could have not blown the shell!" His words were angry, brutal. Fury made his eyes black, his jaw thrust out with hurt.

"It was justice! These dragons were victims, too!" she pled.

"They killed people!"

"They were kidnapped and brought here. They were just trying to get home." She was crying now. Angry that he didn't understand. Disappointed that the only person who knew what she'd just gone through somehow didn't understand. "I had to weigh it out. I had to think about the injured parties – and who might still be injured, and I had to choose the most just choice I could. Sometimes the Real Law doesn't line up with what we think should happen."

"Those are just stupid excuses to justify what you did." Pain swallowed his expression, leaving it drawn and agonized. He wrapped his arms around his head as if he could block out the sight and sound of her. "You've ruined everything. You've freed them all! Marielle, you just destroyed the world! After everything – every sacrifice." He was gasping now and she almost thought he might be close to sobbing. "Marielle, I gave up my eye!"

"I know." Her voice was small. The light was growing brighter as the dragons woke and began to rise from where they had completely encompassed the city.

The sounds of their movements were so loud that she had to strain to hear Tamerlan. Was that Jhinn calling to her? It was so faint she wasn't sure if it was her imagination.

"I gave up my sanity." He lowered his arms so that his hands were planted firmly on the ground, his head hanging down so that it looked like he was going to retch.

Marielle sank to the ground in front of him, on her knees now, too.

"They're going back to their world, Tamerlan. They aren't staying here. We can send them all back to where they came from and all this – this killing and death and blood magic – it will end."

"How do you know?" he wasn't looking at her. It was hard to hear his voice.

"They told me."

"You're madder than I am, Marielle." He choked out a humorless laugh. "Don't you know, the voices in your head are all liars? Mine are. They lie to me all day long. But *I* don't listen to them."

"Don't you?" Sometimes she didn't know if it was him or his voices that made the choices. Sometimes she didn't know if she knew him at all. Even though she'd been in his mind. Even though she'd seen him as a child. Even though she thought she might be falling in love with him.

"I don't –"

His voice faltered like he wasn't sure, either. She knelt on the ground in front of him as the noonday sun rushed to fill the dead city. Snow was drifting down in tiny diamond flakes, swirling around them as the shadows – not clouds, she was sure, but dragons – swirled above.

"At some point, you have to trust someone."

"Not dragons," he spat. "Not Legends."

She reached for his face but he jerked away, shoving her hand to the side. She flinched, feeling the sting of rejection so deeply that it cut through the magic scent around her. Suddenly, she was smelling him – golden and addictive, honey and cinnamon and shattered hope in blueberry blue and aching failure in bitter mustard yellow. And all of that was streaked through with rage that smelled of pitch – but that rage wasn't him. It was tinged with Elderflower – with insanity and Legend. She could almost imagine what he would be like if he'd never smoked the spice

261

and opened the Bridge. He'd be all the good things she loved about him and none of this brokenness.

But as his lower lip trembled in the bright light, as he shied away from her touch like a wounded animal that very vulnerability made him so human – so precious that she wanted to cup him in her hands like a bird with broken wings and keep him tucked away safe.

"Tamerlan?" he flinched at her voice, shaking his head. Bitter tears leaked from his eyes and the scent of Elderberry was strong.

"I killed so many to keep them down. I shed so much blood. When I found them here, I knew it had to be that way. That I'd been right to do that."

Did he mean himself or Ram the Hunter?

"It was all the right choice. I made the right choice!" He was yelling now, slamming his fist into the rock again and again until the knuckles were bloody.

"Tam, stop," Marielle said her own lips trembling now. She'd done this to him. He'd been balancing on the edge of sanity and it had been her choice that sent him hurtling over the edge. "Please, stop."

"You ruined it all," he looked up now, his hurt, trembling lips cutting her to the quick. "With one choice you made it all for nothing! All those deaths! All those lives." He wiped his face with his hand, leaving a trail of his own blood across it. "All that blood on my hands."

He looked at his fist like he didn't know why it was a battered mess. He was shaking his head. No, all of him was shaking.

The world was shaking.

A wind tore across the platform, sweeping the light snow across them so fast that the ice particles stung her cheeks and she had to close her eyes against them. When she opened them, Tamerlan hadn't moved except to grit his teeth. He was shaking all over, shaking his head wildly as if he couldn't compose his thoughts.

"Nothing. Nothing. Nothing," he muttered and with every word he said, her heart seemed to shred.

She'd thought she'd made the right choice. She'd been sure of it.

Until now.

She looked up into the sky, at the swirling dragons high above. There was no more mountain over the city. The mountains all around it seemed low and jagged. She could no longer pick out tails or heads or legs.

But they weren't flying away, were they? The portal was still there – hard to see in the noonday sun. The waters still gushed from it like a flood. But the dragons were in the sky, circling, with no sign of leaving the world at all.

A chill of fear ripped through her and she gasped, trembling now, too.

Had she chosen wrong?

Had she truly destroyed the world?

Captain Ironarm had said that it was these moments – when you worked outside the written law trying to grasp a hold of the Real Law that an officer found out who they truly were. Maybe she had meant that Marielle would find out she was a monster.

"I can't," he said, choking on his own words. "I can't do this anymore. I just can't."

He was gasping in breaths so fast that she thought he was going to pass out, spasming as if something inside him was rebelling. His forehead was pressed against the cold stone, his tears slipping across the rough surface.

She bit her lip. She didn't know how to fix this. She just knew that she had to because the idea of going on without him was unthinkable.

"Tamerlan," she said gently.

He ignored her, gasping as if he couldn't get enough air.

"Tam," she put her hand on his shoulder and he shook it off violently. It hurt to be rejected like that ... again.

Especially now that she realized something she'd been trying to ignore. She was utterly in love with this tortured man.

Maybe she had been for a while now.

If he truly went mad ... she couldn't think of that. She had to hold it together.

"Listen to me, you thick-headed fool! You made these decisions, too. You made these choices, too. You sent people to their deaths! You did that."

He looked up at her with haunted eyes.

"And I pay every day for it." His voice was rough over lips thickened with emotion. "All I ever wanted was to keep you safe, Marielle. All I ever wanted was to keep this," he tapped his own chest. "From happening to you. To keep you sane in a world tearing apart with madness. To keep you whole when I'm splintering apart. Don't you see? It's all been for you. Every bit of it from the first time I fought Etienne's guards to rescue you. Every sacrifice. Every death I've caused was all for you."

She swallowed.

"And it wasn't enough," he choked on the end of his words. He was still fighting some internal battle, still wild in his eyes and scent.

Another gust of wind threatened to knock them over, Marielle swayed, blown across the pillar on her knees until she almost tumbled over the edge. Hands reached out of nowhere, snatching her from the brink and pulling her in a tight embrace.

Tamerlan held her in arms thick with muscle, tucking her in tightly to his chest as the winds battered him.

"Why save me, Tamerlan, when you hate me so much? When I've ended your world?" she asked as she braced against the wind. She wasn't even sure if he could hear her.

"Hate you? Aren't you listening to me? This — all of this was for you. Does that sound like hate? But if you want it to be hate. If you want me to leave you, I will go."

"No!" Her tone was harsher than she intended. "No."

He pulled his cloak around her, tucking her in even tighter so they could look at each other without the wind blinding them.

"There isn't much of me left, Marielle. I can see myself peeling away layer by layer. I can't tell sometimes if it's me or them that's left. I can't tell. You asked me to trust. You should know by now — the only person in all the world I trust is you."

"Then you should trust that I chose the right path."

"Right won't save you from the guilt or the nightmares. It won't save you from crumbling inside." His voice broke for a moment. "I wanted to keep you from that."

"You aren't a god," she said gently, reaching up to stroke his face. He didn't flinch away. "Not even a Legend. You can't save me from having to make choices, Tamerlan Zi'fen. You can't save me from the consequences."

"You're right, I can't." He sounded broken when he admitted it. He was so young when his lower lip trembled like that, when the fear in his eyes shone through, when his overwhelmingly attractive scent stole away all her inhibitions and masks and opened her up to his words so that every one seemed to mold her into the shape of them. "I can only offer you what I have to give — the last shreds of this miserable soul, the last tatters of this broken heart, the last pathetic words of this stuttering tongue."

266

"I take them all. Every one," she said, solemnly, like it was a vow. "I'll never say no to you, Tamerlan. That's my promise. I'll take all your shreds and tatters and someday I'll help you weave them together. Somehow."

WE FLY.

The dragon words in her mind startled her. She'd forgotten there was anyone but her and Tamerlan.

SEND THE REST AND SEAL THE PORTAL. DO NOT FAIL.

She swallowed. "Will you look at something with me?"

"Yes," he whispered, pressing his lips to her hairline. "Will you forgive me?"

"For what?"

"For everything?" His voice cracked.

"Yes."

"Forever?"

"Yes."

She kissed his lips, gently then deeper until she felt like her heart was tangling with his in knots that couldn't come undone. She pulled away after long minutes, gasping. Her desperate reluctance to keep going was mirrored in his eyes.

She asked again, "Will you look?"

He nodded, but his gaze was locked on her, like a starving man watching food just out of reach. She pulled the cloak aside, blushing as his intense gaze never left her.

She looked out and up. The winds tore at her and the snow shredded her skin – made strong and violent from the passing of dragon after dragon over their heads as the dragons dove one by one into the portal.

"Look," she said, with a ghost of a smile on her face.

He tore his gaze from her for long enough to look up and the stunned hope on his face made her heart soar.

"This promise," she said, "was kept. The voices in my head weren't lying to me."

They were silent a long time, just watching, watching, watching as the dragons left their world.

"Then it's over?" he asked. "All over?"

"Not yet. There's more that needs to be done."

"What?" His gaze watched her with obsessive hope. She felt a tingle in her belly as she realized what that was – love. Love from a man whose gorgeous scent was tangled with madness and fury.

"I can't tell you what we're doing next, Tamerlan. Not with those Legends in your head. You're just going to have to trust me. And you're going to have to help."

He was nodded and he tried to smile – though his smile was as broken as he was. "All my tatters, Marielle. They're all yours."

EPILOGUE

TAMERLAN

Tamerlan watched as the last dragon from the mountains dove through the portal, seeming to almost swim into the current of the waters still pouring out of it.

Wrong! This is all wrong! Ram screamed in his mind. He hadn't stopped raving since the first dragons began to plunge into the portal. But shouldn't he be glad about this? It was ridding the world of some of the dragons. *But not all. Never all. You will still have to deal with the ones on the plains, and for that, you will need to make avatars. And you will start with the little witch who blew that shell.*

Tamerlan tried to force him aside, but it was impossible to get Ram out of his thoughts anymore. Even now as his own heart bent to every movement of Marielle, as his own eyes wanted to linger on her forever, as his own feet wanted nothing more than to follow her, rebellion brewed in his mind.

Ram was strong and growing stronger by the moment. And if Tamerlan didn't find a way free of him, then eventually Ram would be even stronger than the love he felt for the girl with the purple eyes.

"Should you close that portal?" he asked Marielle.

"I can't yet," she said, taking his hand. "Come on, we have to go."

"Where are we going?"

"To the Five Cities of the Dragonblood Plains," she said.

Perfect! Ram crowed. *We'll make her an avatar there and bind the dragon you brought to the mountains. I'm ready.*

"I think I should stay here," Tamerlan said, nervously.

"In this dead city?" Marielle asked.

He only shook his head, worried by his trembling hands. Maybe he should smoke anyhow. Maybe it would call one of the other Legends. Any of them would be better than Ram all the time.

Yes! Smoke! Ram sounded excited.

Or maybe it would deliver the last of him into the Hunter Legend's hands.

Marielle led him to Jhinn in the gondola below. Jhinn's eyes were bright with unshed tears. Tamerlan looked at him with puzzlement and at Etienne who sat in the boat too, a barely suppressed rage in his eyes.

"Where is Rajit?" Marielle asked, worry in her voice.

"He took Etienne's boat through the portal," Jhinn said, excitement and longing in his eyes. "It worked. He went on with the dragons."

"And you remained," Marielle said with compassion in her voice. "You could have gone, too."

He shook his head, looking at Tamerlan with an expression Tamerlan couldn't read.

"We're not done here yet," Jhinn said. "You and I have more work to do, Marielle."

"And is anyone going to tell *me* what that work is?" Etienne asked. His eyes were clear of Legend. He didn't look like he was going to attack Tamerlan right now – though he watched Tamerlan with wary eyes – the same way that Tamerlan was watching him.

"Not yet," Marielle. "Right now, you'll just have to trust us."

"When, then?"

"As soon as we can," she said with a sigh. "For now, grab an oar. It's a long way back to the plains."

Without the protection of the dragons, it was also a cold way back to the plains. And as the winter winds blew the snow around them Tamerlan thought of the cities below and the fast they'd be having over Winterfast. They had no idea what their history really was. They had no idea of the sacrifices that had been made ... or the ones still to be made.

He shivered despite the noonday sun and watched Marielle like the moon watched the earth – forever outside its reach, and yet forever the guide of its path. He would just have to trust her. If he dared. And hope he didn't lose the last of himself before she succeeded in saving them all.

BEHIND THE SCENES:

USA Today bestselling author, Sarah K. L. Wilson loves spinning a yarn and if it paints a magical new world, twists something old into something reborn, or makes your heart pound with excitement ... all the better! Sarah hails from the rocky Canadian Shield in Northern Ontario - learning patience and tenacity from the long months of icy cold - where she lives with her husband and two small boys. You might find her building fires in her woodstove and wishing she had a dragon handy to light them for her

Sarah would like to thank **Eugenia Kollia** for her incredible work in proofreading this book. Without her big heart and passion for stories, this book would not be the same.

Sarah has the deepest regard for the talent of her phenomenal artists – **Francesca Baerald** who designed the gorgeous map for this series and Lius Lasahido and his team at **Polar Engine** who created the gorgeous cover art that accompanies this book. Without their work, it would be so much harder to show off this story the way it deserves!

www.sarahklwilson.com

CPSIA information can be obtained
at www.ICGtesting.com
Printed in the USA
BVHW041043290421
606132BV00003B/549